YOU, ME, AND OUR HEARTSTRINGS

YOU,
ME,
AND
OUR
HEARTSTRINGS

Melissa See

SCHOLASTIC PRESS
NEW YORK

CONTENT WARNING:
This book contains depictions of ableism, anxiety attacks, familial emotional neglect, religious bigotry, and discussions of mental health. Please take care of yourself if you aren't ready to read this content. Daisy, Noah, and I will be here when you are.

Library of Congress Cataloging-in-Publication Data available

ISBN 978-1-338-79029-0

10 9 8 7 6 5 4 3 2 1   22 23 24 25 26

Printed in Italy   183

First edition, July 2022

Book design by Yaffa Jaskoll

To the friends who have helped me thrive:

TIA BEARDEN,

for our house in Tennessee and so much more.

JESSICA LEMMONS,

for the hug in Grand Central and the

hot chocolate at Max Brenner's.

MICHELLE MOHRWEIS,

for the late-night chats and being my rock.

I love you beyond words.

YOU, ME, AND OUR HEARTSTRINGS

CHAPTER ONE
DAISY

I stumble into the orchestra room after fifth-chair violinist—
and ever-present thorn in my side—Beaux Beckworth sticks his
leg out across the doorway.

"Sorry, Differently Abled." He tries to sing the nickname
he's had for me our entire four years at this academy, but Beaux
is the sort of person who doesn't even tune his strings properly.
So, he can't exactly carry a tune, either.

"Ha." I smooth down the skirt of my long-sleeved paisley-
patterned dress as cerebral palsy makes a muscle spasm crawl up
my left leg. "You're so funny, using my initials like that."

I hurry across the linoleum floor to the storage room, where
all the violins, violas, basses, and cellos are kept.

Beaux mumbles something about me being second chair, but
before I even push through the door, I hear another voice: It's low,
like the G string on my own violin that's waiting for me inside.

"Are you okay?" Turning on my heel, I meet Noah Moray's eyes and do a double take. Beneath a head of dark brown hair, they're as blue as the forget-me-nots Ma had in stock at her flower shop last month, even behind tortoiseshell glasses.

Noah is the first-chair cellist, and probably the most talented person at this academy. He also rarely talks to anyone.

I've heard him play hundreds of times. But that doesn't mean I'm immune to how brilliant a musician he is.

Or that I'll admit how much I like hearing his voice. Same as the music he plays, it makes my stomach flutter each time I get to listen. Not that I'd ever *tell* Noah this, of course.

"Yeah." I swallow past a slight lump in my throat. My heart thrums in my chest, and my cheeks warm with a blush. "I'm all right."

I quickly duck into the storage room, grab my violin case from its cubby, and rush back to my seat.

"Hello, everyone!" our conductor trills, actually hitting the notes, unlike Beaux. Ms. Silverstein is one of the youngest teachers at the academy, but also one of the most skilled. She played Éponine on Broadway for a season and performed with the Opera Orchestra of New York.

We chorus our hellos back to her, and she perches on the edge of her desk. "First, I want to congratulate you all on a spectacular run of *Fiddler on the Roof*. You were all amazing. Now . . ." She claps her hands, beaming. "It's time to talk about the winter holiday concert!"

Murmurs erupt around the room. The Manhattan Academy of Musical Performance's winter holiday concert is the biggest event of the year, where the band, musical theater, and orchestra students get to take the stage for the night. It's a chance to showcase our skill to the public, music conservatory professionals, and principal conductors. It could be my one shot at getting into Juilliard.

I shift in my seat. Juilliard's my dream. I sent in my prescreening audition back in September. I'm not fooling myself; even on the off chance I did get accepted, my family would never be able to afford the tuition. But this is my chance for a Juilliard faculty member to see me as a skilled disabled violinist—instead of the charity case who got accepted to this school on a scholarship because of my disability.

Maybe that would be enough to earn me a live audition.

I glance across the room at Noah, who's watching Ms. Silverstein with rapt attention, clutching the neck of his cello. Noah's from one of the most illustrious music families in all of New York City. Combined with him being a prodigy? He could probably just walk right into my top-choice college.

That thought makes a kaleidoscope of butterflies flutter in my stomach.

Besides, Noah just looks so handsome, so intense when he plays, creating beautiful music with every press of his strings, every stroke of his bow . . .

"The concert is going to be on December eleventh this year."

Ms. Silverstein's voice brings me back to the orchestra room. "We're, of course, performing a song as an orchestra. But before we dive into options, there is another component." She hops off her desk, walks around to the back of it, pulls open a drawer, and takes out a clipboard. A hush settles over us. "As you know, every year musicians from the orchestra, band, and musical theater are selected to perform duets. There are only four duets, so being chosen is huge.

"I have the duet assignments right here." Our conductor's smile sends another wave of whispers across the room. My best friend, Mazhar Tilki, leans over to say something to me, but I don't quite catch it. My left hand contracts around my bow frog instead.

"Are you ready?" Ms. Silverstein tucks a strand of dark brown curls behind her ear. We say yes, and she clears her throat. "In order of performance: Mazhar Tilki and Eric Zhao."

"Mazhar!" We wrap each other up into a quick hug amid the applause. But it's no surprise he got picked. He's the first-chair violinist and the best one at this academy. From across the room, cellist Eric cups their hands around their mouth and yells to Mazhar: "Ready for this?"

"Absolutely!" Mazhar replies.

Ms. Silverstein moves on down her list, but I tune her out—it's not like I'll be picked anyway. My best friend getting a spot is enough for me.

"And lastly!" she says. "Daisy Abano and Noah Moray."

I'm almost positive she did not just say my name.

My name and Noah's.

Together.

"Daisy!" Mazhar cheers as the orchestra applauds again. "We're both performing a duet!"

Warmth rushes through my whole body at his words, like hearing it from him made it feel real. I grin at him, then down the length of my violin, a blush painting my cheeks. Raising my head, I look for Noah. His eyes are already on me, like they were minutes ago. But he doesn't seem excited. He appears . . . stoic. Like he already knew he'd get selected.

Of course he would, I tell myself. *He's one of the best musicians I've ever seen. And I get to play with him. Finally, I get to show people my talent.*

"All right!" Ms. Silverstein sings, commanding our attention to the front of the room again. "You'll have until this Friday, November sixth, to choose a duet piece and bring it to me for approval. Those of you performing a duet, go off with your partner to any quiet part of the orchestra wing for the rest of the period," she instructs. "Get to know each other better, brainstorm ideas, and don't forget to exchange phone numbers! Be sure to take a packet before you go." She arranges four piles of paper at the front of her desk, one for each instrument. "I've made a list of some possible songs to perform as an orchestra. Your homework is to practice them tonight. Everyone else, let's run through scales and practice them now."

Mazhar and I get up from our chairs, congratulating each other as we join the throng of students grabbing packets. He leaves with Eric, and I walk over to Noah, who's standing next to the line of cellists.

"Should we go to the stage?" he asks.

"Sounds good."

We head out of the orchestra room through the stage's double doors, passing the bulletin board filled with colorful advertisements for the band's field trip to the National Jazz Museum and the winter semiformal next month. The empty auditorium is cool and dark.

My left foot snags on the floor, sending me stumbling into Noah's back. "Ow." I grimace. "I'm sorry."

I'm too embarrassed to meet Noah's eyes, so I watch his sneakers as he turns around to face me. "Are you okay?"

"Yeah." I almost don't look up at him. I don't want to find pity or confusion in his eyes. But instead, he's just watching me, his brow furrowed like I'm a difficult bar of music he hasn't figured out yet. I find I like that; it's preferable to the looks I get at church. "It's just a cerebral palsy thing. So, uh . . ." I clear my throat. "This is amazing." I smile over at him as we sit down, placing the packets onto the music stands. "Are you excited?"

"Yeah." Noah tries to return my smile, but his eyes stray over to his cello instead. "This is a big opportunity. Should we run through scales first? Then play the pieces Ms. Silverstein picked?"

"Sure." My smile falters a little, but I try to focus on how we'll be performing together in a little over a month, right here on this very stage.

On how I get to perform with the best musician in this academy.

I tuck my violin beneath my chin and raise it up as Noah assumes first position—his left pointer finger close to his cello's scroll, his middle finger a short way beneath.

That's when I notice he has Band-Aids wrapped around calluses that dominate each finger.

My own fingers shiver against my strings, sending tiny notes pinging around the stage. I find myself wondering: Exactly how much *does* Noah practice for his calluses to break like that?

"We should do a Bach concerto arrangement for both our instruments," Noah says after we finish the final piece in the packet. "It would be the most intelligent choice."

"Bach?" I repeat. Noah glances up at me, his eyes narrowed. "I mean, we could, but there are so many other arrangements we could do, too. I was thinking something more contemporary with just as much impact. Or we could take on Broadway."

Music exists outside of eighteenth-century Germany. He has to know this.

"We need to think about what's in our best interests," Noah says. "About what would impress the audience." He waves his bow at the empty house, making the hair on the back of my neck stand up. It's like all those plush blue seats are watching us—judging us—before they're even filled with people. "I'll arrange a Bach concerto with my cello and your violin."

"What?" My heart pounds in my ears like allegro, and I can't put my thoughts together fast enough. "Wait. Shouldn't we talk about this? We're supposed decide on our duet together."

"It'll just be easier if you let me handle this," Noah murmurs as the bell rings out in the hallway.

He exits the stage before I can say anything.

CHAPTER TWO
NOAH

My fingers have been itching beneath my Band-Aids the entire ride on the Q train home.

Once I'm aboveground on Seventy-Second Street, my cello case bounces between my shoulder blades as I walk past brown and khaki-colored buildings, and trees kept in small stone fences. Their branches are weighed down by orange leaves even though it's almost winter. Usually, the sound of the leaves rustling in the wind is one of the only things that can stop my heart from pounding in my ears or my thoughts from racing. But right now, it isn't working.

"Ow." I unclench my left hand as I hit the button for the penthouse in the elevator of my building. My fingers must've been digging into my skin without my noticing. Little red crescent moons blossom across my palms.

I'll need to replace the bandages when I get upstairs.

The instant I open the door to my apartment, I hear the familiar whistle of the kettle and my dad's voice booming from the kitchen. He makes a pot of tea whenever anyone is on their way home. It's a tradition he brought with him when he emigrated from Scotland.

"Noah!" he greets me merrily as he and my mom sidestep down to me. Dad's built like a mountain and Mom easily hides behind him. "Put your cello away. Your cuppa is almost ready, and Douglas will be here soon."

"Douglas is coming?" My stomach swooshes. I'd been planning on telling Mom and Dad about the duet over dinner, but I wasn't picturing my oldest, wildly successful brother sitting at the table, too.

"Your mum is convinced the boy isn't feedin' himself right." Dad chuckles as Mom, who's over a foot shorter than him, playfully smacks his arm. "Even though he's now . . . How old, Mackenzie?" He gazes down at her like she's hung the moon, same as always, smiling beneath his full reddish beard.

She adjusts her glasses before curling into him. "Thirty," she murmurs. "Douglas is thirty, Lewis."

"Aye." Dad sighs, kissing the top of her head. "I must've forgotten, eh?"

At that moment, our Scottish terrier, Haggis, realizes I'm home and barrels down the hall to say hello, yapping at my ankles. I crouch down—which isn't easy to do with a cello on my back—and scratch him behind the ears.

"I'll take him out," I offer. It'll give me a minute to think about how I'm going to announce my duet now that Douglas is going to be here.

"Don't be silly, love." Mom disentangles herself from Dad. "I'll do it. You just got home. Go put your cello away, okay?"

We walk back down the hall together. Bright autumn sunlight bounces off the skyscrapers outside and into our apartment. It's beautiful but does nothing to calm my heart thrumming beneath my ribs.

I need a minute to myself.

As Mom gets Haggis's leash and debates which one of his tartan coats he should wear, I duck down the opposite hallway, heading to the practice room.

The walls are covered in framed family photographs. Some are my older brothers' weddings, but most are of us dressed in black and performing on various stages with our instruments.

Even though I see these pictures every time I walk down this hallway, they still make my chest feel tight.

In addition to performing at Carnegie Hall, Douglas is a violinist in the pit orchestra for *The Phantom of the Opera*. Gavin is currently the youngest violist in the Royal Scottish National Orchestra. Since I'm the youngest, I am reminded of my brothers' perfection every day when I pass these pictures. And even though I've been a cellist since before I knew the alphabet, I doubt I will ever measure up.

I duck into the practice room to get away. It has gleaming

hardwood floors like the rest of the apartment, with floor-to-ceiling windows that overlook the Upper East Side. But Manhattan beyond the glass isn't what's most impressive about it.

It's our collection of string instruments, all carefully secured in cases and resting on racks. I can almost hear the low, mournful notes of Mom's violas, the deep tones of Dad's cellos.

Instantly, I'm flooded with memories: Dad letting me feel the vibrations of his cello strings as he played; how he taught me as soon as I learned the names of the strings themselves; how excited the whole family was to have yet another Moray musician. Although what else could they expect?

So, no pressure about my own future in music or anything.

As I slide my cello case off my shoulder, my bandaged calluses press against the strap, and I hiss at the pain.

You would think I'd be used to the way calluses feel when they tear open from the pressure my fingers put on the strings. That I'd learn my lesson, that it'd be as easy as running through scales, like I did with Daisy this afternoon.

But apparently, it isn't. Not when you've been left with a music legacy so vast and impossibly impressive that you have no choice but to push yourself harder, practicing until the sun comes up and your skin splits open.

You have to match their skill, my brain echoes. *You have no choice. Thanks a lot, Douglas and Gavin.*

After I place my cello onto a rack, I go to the kitchen. My dad stops puttering around, the bottle of honey shaped like a bear in his hand, and gestures to the cabinet next to the range hood. "What color mug?"

When I don't say anything—thoughts of my brother, my duet with Daisy, and my future still swirling around in my mind—he says, "Blue mugs it is, then."

Mom's the one who assigned the color of mugs to certain conversations: Red for life-changing ones. Green for happy ones. Yellow for casual ones. And blue for coaxing me to talk. Incidentally, it's my favorite color.

"Sure." I move the step stool out of the way and reach for the mugs, while Dad gathers the tea bags.

"Everything all right?" he asks once we're both seated at the island with steaming mugs in our hands. The question is quiet, like he doesn't want anyone to overhear.

Mom and Haggis are currently fifty-seven floors below us, but still.

"Yeah." I take a sip, letting the warm tea and honey reach all the way to my fingertips. "My fingers are bothering me. That's all."

Dad's brow knits. But music-related injuries are like falling off a bike for my entire family, so he doesn't get on my case about my broken calluses. "We can change the bandages after we finish our tea." He smiles then, his eyes bright and blue like mine, Gavin's, and Douglas's. "They didn't look all that bad last night. They'll heal soon."

Until I rip them open again.

• • •

Haggis's claws scrabble on the floor when he hears Douglas's voice through the intercom. He tears down the hallway, already waiting for one of his favorite humans to arrive.

The whole first floor of the penthouse is filled with the delicious smell of chicken, potatoes, cream, peas, and parsley as stew simmers on the stove. After Dad changed my bandages, Mom assigned me to chopping carrots, cucumbers, and tomatoes for a side salad. The rhythmic motions of slicing them with a knife at least give me something other than music to focus on for a little while.

"Douglas!" Mom squeals, opening the door once he knocks. "Oh, it's so good to see you!"

Douglas and his husband, Levi, live in the Theater District, about twenty minutes away. Better than Gavin, who lives across the Atlantic. But Mom still acts like Douglas crossed a body of water to get to us, which makes me smile down at the cutting board.

I hear the slap of Dad seizing Douglas in a hug behind me, and soon Douglas wraps his arms around my shoulders.

"Hey, little brother." His deep voice thrums in my ear. All the Moray men are six feet or taller, but Douglas still enjoys reminding me that I was born last.

"Hi." I put down the knife and turn around, smirking as we hug.

"This smells amazing, Mom," Douglas says, bringing down plates from the cabinet closest to the sink.

"Thank you." Mom glows, getting drinking glasses.

Dad grabs a bottle of white wine from the chiller on the counter and jokes about how Mom believes no one can feed her sons like she can.

The four of us settle around the glass dining table just outside the kitchen—each with a warm bowl of chicken stew, a plate of salad, and wine for everyone but me. A crystal vase filled with a portion of the sunflowers my parents gave me for *Fiddler on the Roof* sits in the center of the table.

For the first time all day, I notice there is no tension in my shoulders. Sitting around the dinner table, listening to the music of my family laughing and chatting, the smell of the food, it all feels like a sigh of relief.

Douglas scoops some sauce-soaked chicken and potato onto his spoon, saying: "So Rachel picked you to perform a duet, huh?"

I almost choke on my food.

"She *told* you?" I ask as our parents gasp.

Douglas and Ms. Silverstein went to Juilliard together. So as awkward as it is for my brother to be friends with my orchestra conductor, I know they've been friends for longer than I've attended the MAMP.

"What?" Douglas eats what's on his spoon, adjusting his horn-rimmed glasses next. "Of course she told me that my brother is going to be onstage for the school's biggest concert."

"Noah!" Mom claps her hands together over her plate.

"Congratulations! This is excellent! Remember when Douglas was picked?"

Barely? I was four when he was a senior. But his prowess on the violin was obvious to anyone who heard him, even then.

Which makes what little stew I've eaten so far suddenly spoil in my stomach.

"He was perfect," Dad continues, wiping cream sauce from his beard. "So was Gavin when he was picked." He smiles at me, Mom peeking over his arm to match his grin.

"You will be, too." Mom reaches out her hand to squeeze my arm, pressing a kiss to my temple.

"Of course! We have no doubts about that." Dad's eyes gleam. "Who's your duet partner?"

"Daisy Abano," I say. "She's a violinist." A pretty one, with rosy cheeks and brown eyes that perfectly match the braid she wears over her right shoulder.

Douglas takes a sip of wine. "Ah, the superior instrument!" He grins.

I eat another spoonful of stew. Peas pop on my tongue, and thankfully, talk turns to Gavin's newborn baby, Ava. We're all meeting her for the first time when we fly to Scotland for Christmas.

We go every year—and for a month in the summer, too. The excitement of our new family member keeps the conversation off me as Douglas doles out slices of Junior's raspberry swirl cheesecake after dinner.

But I can't focus on the conversation. All I can think about is the duet. How I told Daisy I'd choose the piece we'd perform. I know I should've listened to her more. This is a duet, after all. We should both agree on what we play. I guess maybe a Mozart piece could work, too. But a contemporary piece? What is she thinking? This concert is too important for us to make any mistakes.

Because not getting accepted to Juilliard next fall? That isn't an option.

NOVEMBER 2

Daisy (8:09 p.m.): Can we talk about our duet piece, please? We should agree on one.

NOVEMBER 3

Noah (6:32 a.m.): Bach or Mozart?

Daisy (7:07 a.m.): They're both hugely important to classical music.

Noah (7:09 a.m.): So, you see my point.

Daisy (7:11 a.m.): I see it, but I don't agree with it.

Noah (7:11 a.m.): Why?

Daisy (7:13 a.m.): Because you're ignoring every other genre of music we can pick from. Strings can do more than Bach and Mozart.

Noah (7:19 a.m.): They can. But that doesn't mean doing that is the smartest option. Trust me. We need to be intelligent about this.

Daisy (7:22 a.m.): And we can be.

Noah (7:23 a.m.): So, pick between the two composers.

Daisy (7:23 a.m.): You're impossible.

Noah (7:25 a.m.): I'm realistic.

NOVEMBER 4

Noah (7:37 a.m.): Why not a Bach piece?

Daisy (7:38 a.m.): Don't we have enough of those in our audition repertoires?

Noah (7:40 a.m.): Yes, and for good reason! They show our skill.

Daisy (7:43 a.m.): Doing something surprising and innovative would showcase our skill, too. Mazhar and Eric are working on an arrangement from an anime opening.

Noah (7:48 a.m.): . . .

Noah (7:49 a.m.): For the biggest event of the year?

Daisy (7:55 a.m.): Don't discount their talent like that.

Daisy (7:57 a.m.): What about "Seasons of Love" from Rent? It has a lot of trills we can play around with.

Noah (7:59 a.m.): This concert is a really big deal. You really think a show tune is good enough?

Daisy (8:02 a.m.): There's more to music than composers who've been dead for centuries, you know.

Noah (8:05 a.m.): Not to Juilliard faculty or principal conductors.

Noah (8:05 a.m.): You don't understand this world the way I do. Just trust me.

300 likes

mampedu

Introducing our senior orchestra students who will be performing duets at our annual winter holiday concert!

Aubreydelli

I'm so excited for the concert!

Daniel_Mateo

Congrats to everyone chosen! This year's concert is going to be amazing.

e7string

You picked Daisy Abano because she's disabled, right? That's nice of you!

SEE MORE COMMENTS

CHAPTER THREE
DAISY

The heavenly smell of yufka dough, peppers, tomatoes, and meat, mixing with the sugary sweetness of desserts, fills Café Istanbul, the restaurant Mazhar's parents own. Turkish music plays from speakers hidden inside huge arrangements of pink tulips and purple crocuses. It isn't enough to drown out the noise of Times Square right outside, but few things can quiet the ever-present tourists or the chaos of Broadway.

Or the frustration simmering between my ears.

"This duet is impossible," I announce. "*Noah* is being impossible!"

"C'mon, Daisy." Mazhar moves a sweep of brown hair out of his eyes and drapes his arm around his girlfriend, Amal Shah. His fingers rest near her purple hijab. Amal's brown skin tinges pink, and they share a quick smile.

Mazhar and Amal have been together since our eighth-grade

winter semiformal when we all went to the same middle school. They're adorable; they even have a Pinterest board where they're planning their wedding.

I'm serious.

"It can't be that bad." Amal's brow scrunches as she leans across the table to hold my hand. Her fingers are warm and soft between mine. "You've liked him forever."

"For four long, arduous years," Mazhar adds, pitching his voice high, "you have silently pined for the first-chair cellist of our orchestra. But you don't need to pine anymore. You have an opportunity now!"

"No." I press my left hand to my face and let my spastic fingers spider across my forehead. "I don't. Besides, if you think I would play whatever he wants just because he is cute, you don't know me. We're duet partners who can't agree on anything. Look." Letting go of Amal's hand, I open my text messages with Noah, sliding my phone across the table.

Mazhar and Amal scoot close together to peer down at my phone.

"He wants to go classical for the duet?" Mazhar looks up at me before slicing into his revani. A tiny mountain of pistachios crumbles into the lemon syrup, and cake crumbs dribble onto the front of his maroon sweatshirt. "And you want to make it modern?"

"Exactly." I copy him. The syrup is both tart and sweet, the pistachios crunchy and earthy on my tongue. "It's like he doesn't want to hear other options. He thinks he knows what's best and I may as well not even be there. What should I do? It's not like I can perform with someone like that."

"Talk to him," Amal suggests, readjusting her glasses. She coordinates them with her outfits, so today they're chunky galaxy-patterned frames, paired with an ankle-length purple skirt.

"I've tried." I stuff another forkful of revani into my mouth. "Over and over again. He won't hear me. I just—I don't want him to screw up this opportunity for me. I need this to go well."

"I know you don't," Amal says gently. "But I bet he feels the same way. You have to remember: He's an artist, too. We all are. And part of being an artist is talking about our art with others. You know? Maybe you should try to figure out why he's so adamant about choosing something classical. Then you can help him see why it isn't so necessary," she adds.

"You can't expect to perform your duet well if you're always at each other's throats," Mazhar points out.

"You know that," Amal adds, squeezing my hand before taking a bite of her own revani. "Text him right now. Say you want to talk."

I let go of Amal's hand and slide my phone back to me, texting Noah:

Daisy (3:39 p.m.): Hey, can we talk, please?

When the last crumb of revani has disappeared from our plates and we've all finished our sodas, I look at my phone, but the only text is from my mom:

> **Ma (4:07 p.m.):** Dad and I are going to be late at the flower shop. Go next door. They're watching Holly, and they have pot roast for you. Ti voglio bene, Daisy.

"Any luck?" Amal asks as we're all getting our coats back on.

"No, just my parents letting me know they'll be working late again," I say, shrugging. "You know, the usual." My mom and dad work a lot, but they always make sure I have food in my belly. That makes me feel warm inside, even if I wish they were around more.

I check my phone again, my heart fluttering, hoping he answered after all. *You're being ridiculous, Daisy. This isn't one of those romance novels Nonna reads. He's not going to text you back just because you're checking your phone.*

Nothing. I sigh.

When we spill out of Café Istanbul and into Times Square, narrowly avoiding colliding with a person in an off-brand Elsa costume, Amal gives me a quick hug.

"Good luck tomorrow," she says, hopeful, squeezing my shoulders.

•   •   •

Back in Williamsburg, my sister and I are both stuffed with pot roast, veggies, and potatoes. Then I take Holly back to our apartment next door.

"Dizzy?" My baby sister pulls her thumb out of her mouth. She can't pronounce "Daisy" yet because she's only two. My parents tried for years to have another child, but they gave up years before Holly was born in my freshman year. She was a nice surprise.

"Yeah, bean?" I ask, readjusting her in my arms.

"*Moana?*" she requests.

"Sure."

In our bedroom—which is a mix of my anime art prints tacked up on baby-pink walls and Holly's toys scattered all over the carpet—I get her into pajamas. Then, on the couch in the living room, our TV framed by our baby pictures, I start up the movie.

"Mama!" she squeals when our parents walk through the door. "Daddy!" She springs away from the couch, throwing her chubby arms around their necks.

"We're happy to be home, sweetheart." Dad yawns. They smell like damp soil and gerbera daisies, a comforting scent, if only because it means they're home.

"How was everyone's day?" Ma asks, walking over and sweeping me into a tight hug. Her wavy brown hair, same as mine, brushes my cheek. She always takes it down from its usual bun on the train ride home.

"Good."

I'm only partially lying. I haven't even told my parents about being picked for the duet yet. Not because I don't think they'd be excited for me, but because I know they won't be able to come to the concert in the first place. They haven't attended a show at the MAMP since the fall production of *Into the Woods* when I was a freshman. They always say they will. They promise and make plans. But Holly comes first, or work gets in the way. So, I can't see a good reason to tell them about this show.

I'm just tired of watching other students get bouquets of flowers from their families after shows, some of which I even recognize from Ottavia's Flower Arrangements.

Sunflowers, I think suddenly. After shows, Noah's arms are always filled with sunflowers. *Are they his favorite flower?*

"I'm glad." Ma kisses my forehead, bringing me back to the living room. She grabs Holly from Dad. "Your dad has to cover a shift at the store tomorrow," she says. "So, I'll need you to fill in for him at the flower shop. Can you meet me there after school, please?"

"Sure." I crack my knuckles, weary, but grateful I'll get to spend some time with my mom. "No problem."

CHAPTER FOUR
NOAH

The orchestra room is filled with high, frantic notes from the violins; low notes from the violas; resounding notes from the basses; and deep, rich notes from the cellos as we run through "What's This?" from *The Nightmare Before Christmas*.

I smile, drawing my bow across my strings as it closes. Usually, we don't get to play songs as fun and out there as this one.

"All right, everyone!" Ms. Silverstein commands everyone's attention to the front of the room. "Tomorrow is the deadline for you all to choose duet pieces," she continues. "I want to check in with those of you who are performing just to see where you're at."

I stiffen at her words and stare across the room, my eyes on Daisy, who's glaring right back at me.

We haven't agreed on a piece. We've barely been able to have a conversation about it.

Daisy texted me yesterday, but I didn't see it until I was leaving my apartment this morning. I spent all night mulling over concerto options in the practice room until the sky turned pink. I wasn't paying attention to my phone.

"After that, we'll vote on the piece we'll play as an orchestra," she says. "So, will the duet teams come up to see me, please?"

I get up from my chair and walk, not to Ms. Silverstein's desk with the rest of the musicians, but over to Daisy's seat without a word.

"Hi," Daisy mutters, her cheeks blotchy as I sit down next to her. "I texted you yesterday. Are you ignoring me?"

"No, I am not ignoring you, I was busy," I reply. "Practicing. I didn't even see your message until this morning."

"You know something?" Daisy grumbles. "You're sucking all the fun out of this. Not to mention ruining this opportunity for both of us. This isn't . . ." Her left hand balls into a fist on her jeans. "This is a big opportunity for me. It isn't just about you anymore, like it has been for the last four years."

I narrow my eyes. "What the hell is that supposed to mean?"

"You never talk to anyone!" Daisy bursts out, her words making me take a sharp breath. "If you did, you might have actually listened to my options for our duet instead of insisting on Bach!"

"Oh!" I laugh, my voice breaking. "So, I guess the fact that I went over options for our duet until sunrise isn't enough for you? You have no idea how hard I am working, or how much pressure I am under."

"You couldn't have texted me tha—"

"Excuse me?" Ms. Silverstein's voice gently cuts through our argument. Daisy and I jump in our seats, turning to our teacher. We didn't realize she was standing there. "I noticed you two were arguing. Can I step in to mediate?"

Daisy and I nod, too embarrassed to say anything.

Ms. Silverstein nods back, instructing the rest of the class to run through scales, then song options.

Once we pass through the double doors and reach the auditorium stage, Ms. Silverstein folds her hands in front of her dress. A few brown curls are already escaping from the bun piled on top of her head. "Care to explain what's going on?" she asks kindly.

The heat from the lights above our heads wraps around me, and I tug at the red plaid shirt under my sweater, wishing I had worn something lighter instead.

"I'm sorry, Ms. Silverstein." Daisy bows her head.

"You should be, you yelled at me," I point out, completely aware that I sound like a child. Daisy stares up at me, fire dancing in her brown eyes. "It's not my fault we haven't decided on a piece! It takes two to make an argument."

"I wouldn't have argued with you if you weren't being a jerk! And it's impossible to decide on a piece if you can't bother to take time from your precious practice to talk to me!" she retorts.

"So, I'm a jerk now?" I snap. "Why? Just because I think we should—"

"Enough!" Ms. Silverstein clears her throat, stepping backward. I'm a head taller than my orchestra conductor, but right now, I feel like I'm approximately the size of an ant beneath her gaze. "I brought you out here to talk, not argue. Listen. I paired the two of you to perform for a reason, okay? You're both incredible musicians, with brilliant careers ahead of you. Your approach to music is very much the same. Matching levels of passion and drive." My stomach dips, and I glance over at Daisy. She's looking at me, too, but I can't place her expression.

"So, please—" our conductor says, getting cut off when another pair of double doors opens up at the top of the aisle.

"Rachel!" Mr. Castillo, the musical theater director, strides up to the stage. He smiles at her. But when his eyes shift to me and Daisy, he squares his shoulders, clearing his throat. "I—I mean, Ms. Silverstein." She goes pink. Blush reaches the roots of his dark hair as he's suddenly interested in adjusting his succulent-patterned tie. "I wasn't expecting to see you here. What's going on?"

"Well, Mr. Castillo." Ms. Silverstein folds her arms across her chest. "Daisy and Noah seem to be at odds."

"I could hear you yelling from the hallway," Mr. Castillo says, surveying us—not disappointed, but not friendly, either. "Now, I know neither of you are attending this school for musical theater—"

Daisy raises her right hand. "I'm a soprano, actually."

"And I, um." I thread my fingers through my hair. "I'm a baritone? I think?"

Mr. Castillo's eyes soften, and the corners of his mouth quirk upward. "If you have to think, then you don't know your vocal range," he explains. "That aside. Do you prefer to explain yourselves to us or to Principal Loman?" Daisy and I stiffen beside each other. I'm not sure if she's met him before, but I have, after I won gold at the New York State School Music Association festival last year. Hudson Loman is a legend. Before he came to this school, he was the principal violinist for the New York Philharmonic.

And he makes me anxious. I've never been in trouble before, but just the thought of going to his office makes my throat dry and my heart pound in my chest. "We'll talk to you," Daisy says.

"Very well, then." Ms. Silverstein turns on her heel and descends the short staircase off to the side. "So," she says once she and Mr. Castillo are seated in the front row and Daisy and I are sitting onstage, our legs dangling over the edge. "Talk, please."

"We, uh." I tug at my shirt collar again, feeling my Adam's apple bob in my throat. "We haven't been able to agree on a piece."

"We know that's not an excuse," Daisy continues, folding her hands in her lap and glancing over at me. "People from Juilliard will be in the audience. I thought that—"

"Meant something to me?" I finish, biting down on each word. "It does."

"But why are you being so—"

"No." Ms. Silverstein gets to her feet, her heels clacking. "Please don't start arguing again. So, you didn't pick a piece. That doesn't mean you can yell at each other. You need to fix this." She turns to me. "Just like your cello and violin have to find a way to harmonize, so do you."

"Well, um." My voice chooses this moment to crack. "I think performing a classical piece is important."

"But why?" Daisy asks. All the frustration is gone. Instead, she sounds exhausted, and I immediately feel horrible.

I turn away from our conductor to meet her eyes. The lights make them a brighter, richer brown. "Because it's what my brothers did."

A crinkle forms in Daisy's forehead. Neither Mr. Castillo nor Ms. Silverstein says anything. "Noah, what do your brothers have to do with any of this?"

"They're musicians, too," I practically wheeze, wincing at the pressure of my heart beating in my ears. "A violinist and a violist. They even compose their own music. Sometimes it's contemporary, but mostly, it's classically inspired because that's what we've all been trained in." What I don't say is, *I need to be as good as them.*

The silence that rings around us is identical to the kind that happens after the last note in a piece is played. It's loud, somehow filling up the whole auditorium.

Except there is none of the release, the exhilaration that usually comes with it.

Daisy blinks; I blink back.

"Your brothers are composers," she says finally.

"Yeah." I clear my throat. "They have a YouTube channel. The Moray Stage?" They started it when Gavin announced he was getting married and staying in Scotland. Five hundred thousand subscribers love seeing the songs they post every week. They ask me to join sometimes, but I always say no.

Daisy nods. Then she knocks her foot against mine. And only then do I realize how close we've been sitting this entire time.

That thought makes me run my hand through my hair.

"What?" I ask. I can see an idea taking shape in her eyes.

"Noah, why don't we have your brothers compose something for us? We can't agree on a piece, so what if we left it up to them?" She runs her hand along her braid, trying to smile, and I hate myself for thinking about how sweet she looks. I don't have time to think that she—or anyone—is pretty. Except, she is. "Giving them free rein completely?"

My eyebrows rise above my glasses. They'd do it, and probably have it finished in less than a day. "And if they give us a classical piece?"

Daisy sighs. "Then that's what we play. But you aren't allowed to give them any direction. Deal?" She holds out her hand, and I shake it, marveling for a second at how small it is in mine.

The bell rings, and Ms. Silverstein and Mr. Castillo tell us to get to class. After we walk through backstage and hurriedly pack up our instruments in an empty orchestra room, Daisy disappears down the hall, her yellow backpack swinging.

I collide with Beaux Beckworth.

"Hey." He smiles up at me, and I readjust my glasses in response. "So, I couldn't help but overhear that whole thing. You and Differently Abled got special treatment, huh?" Beaux steps backward, his sneakers squeaking on the tile.

"That's not her name." I hate how my voice is just a whisper.

"Being paired up with the special needs girl has its perks, doesn't it?" Beaux snorts.

Every word he says is making my blood boil a few degrees hotter than the last.

My heart pounds in my ears. This hallway is suddenly far too small a space for two people. "You're just jealous you weren't picked," I land on saying. His pupils widen. He must be as surprised as I am that I'm sticking up for Daisy when I've barely talked to her until now. "You know you could be as good as Daisy if you actually tried, but you're lazy. You don't even tune your strings properly."

Beaux scoffs. "Still . . . your own song for the concert." He turns on his heel. "I just hope your partner is up to the challenge."

CHAPTER FIVE
DAISY

My head is still spinning when I get to the flower shop after school. And even though I tell my mom I'm just tired from walking, she points to the stool behind the counter.

"Sit there." She hands me an apron—a bright green one with my name and the store's hand sewn on it in yellow. "You need to rest, so you're on counter duty until we go home, okay? It's sauce night at Nonna and Nonno's." The once-a-week tradition of having spaghetti at my grandparents' apartment is one of my favorite things. Not least of all because it means we actually get to eat as a family.

Ma kisses my cheek, then disappears into the back room, where she does her flower arranging, her usually tidy bun coming the slightest bit loose as she walks.

I'm sitting surrounded by displays of orange gerbera daisies, white calla lilies, and Peruvian lilies in lurid pinks and yellows.

The *Hadestown* Broadway cast recording plays on the speakers next to the bouquet of fresh daisies Ma must have made to put on display.

I'm grateful for the tranquility because Rockefeller Center buzzes just beyond the windows. Even on a weekday, it's flooded with tourists flocking to the ice rink. The tree won't pull in people from all corners of the world until next month, though.

I bury my face in my hands, trying to absorb what's happened: Noah and I are having an original song composed for us. By his brothers. To perform at the winter holiday concert.

It's surreal. I never thought I'd have an opportunity like this.

The bells above the door jingle, momentarily erasing the thoughts from my mind. I lift my head, ready to welcome the customer.

But the words get caught in my throat.

Because Noah is standing in the middle of the shop, a tall portrait of dark hair, a black peacoat, and a red tartan scarf tucked in around his throat.

"Noah," I finally whisper.

"Daisy," he whispers, backing into the door. The bells jangle again, and he peers up at them, almost like he wants to look anywhere but at my eyes. He clears his throat, the sound sharp and hard. "Um. Hello."

"Hi." I tap the countertop to the beat of the song. "What are you doing here?"

"Buying flowers?" Noah meets my gaze. The old wood

floor creaks beneath his sneakers as he steps forward. "I didn't know you worked here."

"My family runs this store." I gesture around, momentarily proud. Nonna Silvia opened this shop soon after she and my mom arrived in the city from Italy. It was Silvia's Flower Arrangements back then. She died a few months after I was born, but Ma keeps her picture in the window display, accompanied by her favorite seasonal flower. Bluebells in the spring. Marigolds in the summer. Asiatic lilies in the fall. And poinsettias in the winter.

"Who are you getting flowers for?" My heart flutters against my ribs. I mean, Noah could have a secret significant other that no one knows about. I run through the faces of students he could have a crush on—

"You, actually."

"Excuse me?" I blink, warmth painting my cheeks. "I—I mean, thank you. But why?"

Noah's pale skin flushes pink now, too. "To apologize. For how I've been acting."

Before I can reply, the door to the back room whips open. "Daisy?" Ma calls, sending shivers down my spine. "I heard the bell. Do we have a customer?"

My stomach sinks down to my shoes. Since my parents still have no idea about the duet, they're clueless about everything going on between me and Noah, too. And explaining either of those things in the middle of our flower shop, in front of him, is not what I had in mind.

"Yeah, Ma." I swallow through the tightness in my throat. "This is Noah."

My mom smiles at him, extending her hand. She smells like chrysanthemums today. "Ottavia Abano."

"Noah Moray." He doesn't miss a beat—he never does—and shakes her hand. "It's nice to meet you, Mrs. Abano."

Ma narrows her eyes, like she's trying to figure something out. "Are you Lewis and Mackenzie's son?" she asks.

"Yes," Noah replies. "They always come here for flowers when I—well, Daisy and I—perform." My fingernails bite into my palm as a muscle spasm snakes down my left arm. *Sunflowers.* "So, I wanted to do the same."

"Well, thank you very much." Ma smiles at him. "What kind of flowers are you looking for?"

Noah thinks for a moment, gazing at the lilies. In his silence, Orpheus sings about marrying Eurydice. The actor's voice is breathy and nervous, yet still strong—like his own.

Then Noah's eyes settle on the bouquet of daisies. Gerbera daisies, black-eyed Susans, and purple coneflowers.

"Daisies, please," he says.

"An arrangement like this?" Ma points to it. He nods. "Who are they for?"

"Your daughter."

Both our cheeks flush pink again.

My mom turns to me so fast, it's a wonder she doesn't break her neck.

"Daisy?" she whispers faintly, holding the tiny silver cross on her necklace. "Do you— Amore, are you dating this boy?"

"What?" I squeak. "No! I'm not— We're not dating."

"It—it's for our duet," Noah splutters, clearing his throat again. "To celebrate our duet for the winter holiday concert next month." Ma looks between us, her brows knitted in confusion. "The academy's biggest event of the year," he clarifies.

I close my eyes for a second, not wanting to see Ma's face when she turns toward me.

"That sounds lovely," she says instead of asking why I never told her. I open my eyes; she's smiling at Noah now, her face smooth. "Noah, I have enough flowers to make you an arrangement just like this one here. I can take care of it now if you can wait a little bit?"

"That would be great, Mrs. Abano."

"Wonderful." She smiles over at me now. "Let me go make that bouquet for you."

Noah waits until my mom disappears into the back room again before he shifts his gaze to mine. "Daisy, can I ask you a question?"

Now that I know that he came here to buy me flowers, hearing my name coming from his lips sounds different.

Warm, gentle somehow.

"Yeah?" *Ignore the flutter in your chest, ignore the butterflies in your stomach. Just because a boy does something nice for you doesn't mean anything bigger is happening.*

"Your mom doesn't know about the concert, does she?" he asks.

"No." I tap along to the beat of the music softy playing. "She doesn't."

"Why?"

"It's complicated," I settle on saying. "My parents don't have a lot of time for me. They aren't like yours."

"But your mom seems nice."

"Oh, she is," I say. "My family is great. It's just that they have to work a lot. And my sister is so little. She's a toddler, so she needs a lot of attention. They haven't been able to come to any of our shows since *Into the Woods*. But it's fine. It doesn't bother me anymore, you know?"

Yes, yes, it does.

Noah's eyes grow wide behind his glasses. He probably can't imagine that his parents wouldn't be waiting for him in the lobby, their arms full of bright yellow sunflowers, after every show. "I'm sorry."

"Thank you." I readjust myself on the stool, my fingernails sinking into my palm again. "Can I ask *you* a question now?"

"Sure." Noah tugs at the scarf around his neck, freeing it from an opening in his coat. The tartan reveals itself to include green checks with white, yellow, and blue lines.

"Why does the kind of music your brothers make matter so much to you?"

"It's complicated," Noah echoes me, sliding his fingers

through his hair. The back-room door opens before he can continue. He shuts his mouth as the door closes behind my mom.

"Here you go." She smiles, handing him the bouquet wrapped in cellophane, tied together with a simple burlap ribbon.

Noah takes his wallet out of his coat pocket, handing Ma his credit card. She swipes it and hands it back to him, along with a receipt, and excuses herself to the back room again.

"Um." Noah's face matches the Peruvian lilies in the shop. "These are for you." He offers me the bouquet, and I take it, the cellophane wrapping crinkling in my arms.

"Thank you." The smell of my namesake floats around us, and Noah steps backward. "Did you choose daisies to be funny?"

Noah smiles at my question. My stomach flips. I've never made him smile before. His hand covers his mouth quickly, but his eyes are still folded at their edges. I ignore the urge to reach across this counter, pull his hand away, and ask him to keep smiling. "Maybe." He takes another step back. "I'll see you at school tomorrow?"

"Tomorrow." I smile back at him, and I swear I hear his heartbeat thrumming.

Noah spins on his heel, crooning, *"Lover, when I sing my song, all the rivers'll sing along . . ."* He *is* a baritone.

Wait.

I get up from my stool, rushing out from behind the counter. The creak of the floor stops him from returning to Rockefeller Center, because he turns to me. "What is it?"

"You know this song?" I ask. He nods. "But you—"

"I never said I didn't *like* show tunes." Noah smiles at me again. Then he disappears into the cluster of tourists and gray November sky.

As if she had her ear pressed to the door and was waiting for Noah to leave, Ma comes back out into the shop. Her fingernails are caked with soil, and she brushes stray petals from her apron.

"Were you listening to us?" I raise one eyebrow at her.

"Well, what did you expect me to do?" She takes a mappina from her apron pocket, scrubbing at the dirt. "A boy comes in and buys you flowers? And then he says you're performing a duet at your academy's biggest concert of the year?" Her forehead wrinkles. "Daisy, why didn't you tell us about any of this?"

The cold air outside seeps in through the draft in the window that we can't afford to fix, raising goose bumps on my skin underneath my sweater. "Because you and Dad have enough to worry about," I respond, hugging myself.

"Well, maybe we are busy, but we still want to hear about all your accomplishments! I'm very proud of you, amore." Ma presses a kiss to my cheek. "I wish you would've told me, but at least now I know, right?"

"Right." I smile at her, and she shoos me back to the stool.

FROM: Douglas Moray-Porter <douglas.lennox.mp@ themoraystage.com>

TO: Noah Moray <noah.moray@mamp.edu>

CC: Daisy Abano <daisy.abano@mamp.edu>

DATE: November 7, 2:00 p.m.

SUBJECT: Duet Completed!

Hi Noah and Daisy,

I've attached both pieces of the duet sheet music, as well as a video of Gavin and me performing it. (We had Isla arrange your cello part, Noah.) Schedule a meetup time and get practicing as soon as you can, since you're behind everyone else.

Good luck!

Douglas

CHAPTER SIX
DAISY

After Mass the next day, I pore over the video and the printout of the sheet music on both trains I take to get to Noah's apartment.

If Noah is the best cellist at our academy, his brother is the best violinist I've ever seen. He plays beautifully, as if his fingers are simply gliding through water instead of up and down strings at the sort of complicated, practiced speed I can only dream of, portraying something as completely effortless when it's the exact opposite.

Plus, the duet is *epic*—equal parts dramatic and tender.

My heart races as I walk past the brownstones on Seventy-Second Street. I've been here before; Amal lives in the same building. The autumn leaves shivering on the trees surrounded by tiny stone fences are the same. The spotless glass doors are the same, as are the burnished intercom, the polished lobby, and sleek silver elevator. But I've never been over to Noah's apartment.

Noah lives in a penthouse. In the wealthiest part of Manhattan. Because of course he does.

Knocking on his door, the simple beat of my knuckles is a drumline that matches the pace of my heartbeat.

"Coming!" Noah calls. "Haggis, watch—" He opens the door a second later, wearing khakis, a navy-blue cardigan, and argyle socks, clutching a squirming mass of hyperactive black fur.

"Hi." I go to wave, but hold my left arm down on instinct, knowing it's already hovering in the air.

"Are you allergic to dogs?" Noah steps backward to let me in, his dog immediately licking his face. "Sorry, I should've asked beforehand."

"No, it's fine." I smile as I take off my sneakers, lining them up on the shoe rack next to the Morays' hall closet. "I've just never really had a pet."

"You can say hello if—if you want." Noah's laugh trickles out as his dog moves from licking his cheeks to stuffing his nose in his ear. "As you can see, Haggis is friendly."

"Haggis?" I repeat, raising an eyebrow as I run my fingers through his fur, chuckling when he starts licking the back of my hand. "You named your dog after . . . What *is* haggis, anyway?"

"Um." The word pops from Noah's mouth as Haggis attempts to climb onto his shoulder. "It's best not to know." He turns on his heel, bringing us to the expansive living room, where his parents are cuddled together watching *RuPaul's Drag Race* on a huge flat-screen TV, a bowl of cheese curls between them, with bright sunlight streaming through the floor-to-ceiling windows.

"Mom, Dad, this is Daisy," Noah introduces me. "Daisy, my parents, Mackenzie and Lewis."

"Daisy!" his dad booms from his place on the overstuffed couch. "Good to meet you, my love. Care for a cup of tea before you start practicing?"

"No, thank you," I say.

"Later," Noah says, putting Haggis on the floor. He makes a beeline for a fluffy plush bed in the corner, curling up like an armadillo.

"Are you sure you won't mind us practicing?" I ask Noah's parents. "We can wait for your show to finish. My mom hates when I practice during *The Hope Baker Hour.*" Hope Baker is this perpetually perky millionaire New York chocolatier/daytime talk show host who has celebrities on to bake random confections and also gives hundreds of thousands of dollars away to everyday deserving people. Ma and Nonna lap it up.

"Is that the talk show where celebrities fail at improving boxed brownie mix?" Noah asks.

"And the *host* always talks like *this!*" I add, impersonating Hope Baker herself.

"We don't mind at all, honey." Noah's mom smiles at me, chuckling. "We won't even hear you. Come out when you want a snack, okay? We're never short on tea and cookies."

"Thank you." Confused, I grin at her, and Noah leads me down a hallway lined with framed photos of him and his brothers.

"What does she mean, they won't even hear us?" I ask.

"We have a practice room." Noah opens a door next to an accent table featuring a crystal vase full of fresh sunflowers. My stomach flips, thinking about the bouquet of daisies we have on our tiny dining table because of him.

Inside is a room perfectly fitted with soundproof panels. Instrument stands filled with cases line the walls, their silver clasps gleaming in the light from the windows overlooking the city below. Two chairs and music stands are already in the center, waiting, along with Noah's cello resting on its endpin, propped up against one of the seats.

"Wow." My eyes flit from the cases to the paneling.

"Yeah." Noah shrugs. "It *is* pretty great, isn't it? It's been here since before I was born. See?" He points to a picture on the wall next to the room. It's his mom, beaming with her viola pressed against her swollen, pregnant belly as she stands in the center of the space. Love is all over her face, and it's hard to figure out if that's from music, her unborn son, or both. I try to imagine my mom looking at me the same way, and the flash of her face tugs at my heart.

"Are you ready?" he asks, jerking me out of my reverie as we walk into the room. I nod, and he closes the door behind us.

After we run through our scales, I lower my violin, balancing it on my lap. The sheet music for our duet is splayed on stands in front of us.

Noah gestures to me. "You first."

My cheeks turn the same shade of pink as my dress, but I study his cello's fingerboard. "You have the first note, though." Swallowing, I lean over to touch his C string.

Except I touch the back of Noah's hand instead.

His pulse beats through his finger, making my heart feel like my strings during allegro—fast, almost too quick to comprehend.

His right hand doesn't have the calluses that are on his left. His fingers are long, smooth, and warm, something that sticks in my brain when mine fall away from them.

"How do you know my first note?" He's whispering, even though no one can hear us. "You don't play cello, too, do you?"

I shake my head. "You know my first note, don't you?"

"A3," he replies faintly. A smile flickers across his face and he moves closer, sending shivers down my arms and thoughts surging through my mind. *We're alone. We're not onstage. We're not in my family's flower shop. We're in his family's penthouse, in their practice room with string instruments that are collectively worth more than an entire year's rent for my apartment. And no one can hear us.*

"Daisy?" His voice cracks, high and tight.

"Sorry." I fall back against my chair, ripping my hand away from his cello as if it just spontaneously combusted. "Wait, I don't even know why I'm apologizing. I—I mean, it's a good thing that we know each other's first notes, right?"

"Yeah." Noah plucks his strings, letting the panels on the walls absorb each note before drawing his bow across his instrument.

I come in next. My bow swims across the strings as my fingers glide up and down the board, movements that pull notes from my instrument filling the room with shivering music that is equal parts high and low, each bar merging seamlessly into the next.

But then my hand tightens around my bow frog in a muscle spasm, turning my knuckles white, and I lower my violin in the middle of the piece.

Noah stops moving his bow across his strings, a low note seeming to reverberate around the room.

"Sorry," I mutter, my cheeks burning as I meet his eyes. "I didn't mean to stumble there."

"Better hope that doesn't happen during our duet." Noah chuckles. "We wouldn't want to screw up our performance."

It feels like the floor has opened up, sending me plunging through the penthouse, all the way down to the street below.

"What's that supposed to mean?" Hating how my voice breaks, I get to my feet. But he's still taller than me when sitting down.

"Daisy." Noah's eyes darken, and he grips the neck of his cello as if it is what's tethering him to Earth. He seems startled by my reaction. "I—I'm sorry. It was a joke."

"Oh." My eyes are hot, and tears are already pricking the bottoms. But I'm not going to cry here. I blow out a breath. "Noah, please don't joke about that."

"I'm sorry," Noah repeats, his voice high again.

"Thank you." I lean forward, the quiet pressing around us. "Do you have any idea what this duet means to me?" My muscles tighten in a way that, for once, has nothing to do with cerebral palsy. "It means my talent as a violinist is being recognized. Not the circumstances that preceded it. Juilliard is not guaranteed for me—my future in music feels so unsure. This is my chance. For once. Plenty of people like Beaux Beckworth never let me forget how lucky I am—"

"Daisy," Noah attempts, "I'm not like that."

"No?" I say. "No one thinks they are. And maybe you aren't as bad." I spread my arms out at my sides, the skirt of my dress brushing against my knees. "Even some of the best of people are *like that*. My priest, Father Benedetti, had the whole church pray for me when I was born, asking God to heal me. There are *dozens* of people just like that in the congregation. They see me as nothing more than the 'inspiring disabled girl' in need of their prayers and their pity. In need of a cure. I see it every Sunday." I swallow the end of the sentence, still trying not to cry, and I narrow my eyes. "I don't need you seeing me that way, too, Noah."

"You can't be serious." Now Noah is on his feet, leaning his cello forward instead of his body. Stepping backward into the chair, I nearly lose my balance. "I don't see you that way. I see you as a musician." His brow crinkles as tears fall down my cheeks, dribbling off my chin and onto my dress.

I cover my mouth with both hands, the fingers on my right hand sticky from rosin.

"I'm sorry," he whispers for the third time. "I—I didn't . . ."

"When people look at you." I drop my hands. "What do they see?"

"Um." Noah's gentle baritone rumbles between us. "I don't know."

"Then I'll tell you." I take a deep breath. "They see a cello prodigy who won gold at NYSSMA. But because I'm disabled, they never see me as a violinist first." Muscle spasms crash through my arms and legs, and I grit my teeth against them. "They see an inspiring disabled girl who plays violin, not a talented, disabled violinist. Even though that's what I *am*."

Noah gazes down at me. He presses the sleeve of his cardigan to my cheek, wiping away a fresh batch of tears as easily as if they were raindrops on his glasses.

It's soft, the way he touches his cello's strings.

I don't want him to take his hand away.

He drops it way too soon. "Daisy, it will never happen again. Let's keep rehearsing."

I shake out my left arm, willing my muscles to loosen and my hand to stop cramping. My body relaxes into itself, and I reposition my violin underneath my chin. People at church who have known me since I was in diapers are never this quick about understanding who I am. And for Noah to understand so simply? It's surprising.

The notes float from my violin and past Noah's ears. The melody dances around the room, violin and cello winding through the air, sinking into our bones and the soundproof panels on the walls.

A beautiful swell of strings only we can hear.

As the song ends in a frenzied vibrato, my braid whips my shoulder from how quickly I play.

And I let the final note—another A3—ring out from my instrument before collapsing into the chair in front of Noah, beaming.

"Wow." I almost laugh instead of speaking, the bright lights above our heads popping across my eyes.

"Wow," Noah agrees. The word makes my gaze snap up to his. His blue eyes are electric, his lips slightly parted, both causing my heart to pound against my ribs. *He's admiring what I just did.*

Our cheeks pink, we play it again—filling up the practice room with enough smooth notes and shivering vibrato that we lose track of time—until there's a knock on the door.

"You've been practicing for well over two hours," Noah's dad tells us from the hall. "Daisy, how do you take your tea, love?"

"Dad." Noah turns on his heel and opens the door. "We need—"

"I'm not listening to you," his dad replies, ruffling Noah's hair and easily looking at me over his head. "You never know when to take a break. We have PG Tips if that changes things. It's a black tea."

"Two spoonfuls of sugar and a bit of milk, please," I tell him, like I drink tea every day and am not just guessing based on how sweet I like hot chocolate. "Thank you, Mr. Moray."

"You're welcome." Noah's dad smiles at me from behind his beard. "C'mon, then. Both of you."

After we're settled with mugs of tea and a plate of cookies, Mr. Moray leaves us at the kitchen island to return to the living room and more competition shows, carrying a tray of tea and cookies for him and his wife.

I look around at the shininess of Noah's apartment. There is a staircase with glass steps. The kitchen is huge, with sleek stainless-steel appliances that still look new, framed by black cabinets and counters, graced with modern silver tiles that seem to reflect the Upper East Side across their surface. Just beyond is a large terrace with planters full of lurid purple delphiniums. I can't help but feel a little bit out of place.

But there are still family photos on the walls, and notes held to the fridge with magnets, along with a whiteboard noting when Haggis needs to be fed. Normal things. Things that make it feel like a real home.

So, I try to focus on those instead. We aren't that different.

Once we've sipped our tea down to the dregs and eaten at least three chocolate chip cookies each, I notice the sky has turned a deep blue outside.

"It's getting late." I hop off the stool. "I should get home."

"Let me help you get a cab," Noah says. A taxi all the way home would cost me a fortune.

"No, that's okay! I have some studying to do on the subway," I say quickly. "When do you want to practice again?"

"Tomorrow?" Noah gets to his feet, and we walk down the hall to the practice room so I can collect my violin. "We're behind everyone else, so we should practice as much as we can."

I nod. He's right. Everyone else has already been rehearsing a week longer than we have. "Should I just come here with you after school?"

"I could go over to your apartment instead," Noah offers.

"No," I say, too fast. Too loud. *Not yet. I'm not ready for you to see my apartment with its tiny kitchen and the bedroom I share with Holly.* "It's okay. You have a practice room, so it's easier here."

I'm not exactly lying.

Trying to ignore how the thought of coming back here makes my heart race, I say goodbye to his parents before heading to the door.

Noah steps forward after I open it. "Can I walk you out?"

"Sure."

I'm grateful he takes a minute to step into his shoes, so that he doesn't see my pink cheeks. We ride the elevator together in a nervous silence. It dings and the doors open, and I am ready to dash out.

"Hi, Daisy!" Amal says, holding Mazhar's hand and

walking over to us. Today, she's wearing a blue floral-patterned hijab, paired with a matching skirt, a cozy yellow sweater, and glasses that sparkle under the lights. Mazhar matches her in a blue plaid button-down, and I wonder if they called each other to coordinate their outfits. "Oh!" She beams, her eyes glittering. "You must be Noah. Right?"

"Yeah." Noah glances between me and my friends.

And soon, Mazhar and Amal are also wearing matching smiles.

"I'm Amal, Daisy's best friend," Amal introduces herself. "And you already know my boyfriend, Mazhar." Mazhar waves at him anyway. She pulls on his arm. "We should get upstairs, Meri Jaan."

"Right, canım." Mazhar smiles at us, letting himself get tugged over to the elevators by his girlfriend. They lean in close, whispering to each other.

"Excuse me?" Noah calls, his voice ringing in the empty lobby. "Can you hold the elevator?"

Mazhar puts his finger on the button, and Noah turns to me. One hand is in his hair, while the other is readjusting his glasses. "I'll, uh." He clears his throat, and I take a step closer to him.

"See you tomorrow?" I finish, not trusting myself to smile believably.

"Yeah." He starts walking backward, his glasses sliding down the bridge of his nose. "See you tomorrow."

I wave at him. He takes his hand out of his hair to wave back, curls now sticking out all around his head. My best friends grin at him as he approaches.

Amal presses the elevator button; I duck outside. Hugging myself against the cold, I grab my phone from my coat pocket, navigating to the group chat I have with Mazhar and Amal:

Daisy (5:35 p.m.): Please don't say anything. 😖

Mazhar (5:35 p.m.): No promises! 😎

Amal (5:35 p.m.): 🙊🙊

CHAPTER SEVEN
NOAH

I'm not exactly well versed in making friends, so I don't know how to jump into a conversation with Mazhar and Amal. I just let the air hang between us in the elevator instead.

A ding signifies that we've passed the third floor, and I clear my throat, trying to figure out how I can inconspicuously wipe my palms on my khakis.

"Did you want to say something?" Mazhar's voice is warm and easy, like we've been friends for our entire lives. A stab of envy worms its way through my stomach.

"Oh." I shake my head. "No."

Amal smiles at me, her eyes crinkling behind her glasses. "How's rehearsing going?" she asks. "What song did you pick?"

"An original piece my brothers composed," I explain, watching the LED numbers on the elevator's wall tick upward the higher we go. "It's . . ." I scrub at my hair, thinking back to a few hours ago—not when Daisy and I played, oddly enough. But instead, when she told me about how people see her, and how I put my hand on her cheek to wipe her tears away.

"Good?" Mazhar finishes.

"Yeah." I drop my hand, nodding. "How is yours?"

Beaming for the rest of the ride up to Amal's floor, Mazhar tells me about rehearsing, how much fun he and his duet partner are having.

I'm so grateful for his voice filling up the elevator that the silence feels strange after they leave.

I head right into the kitchen to help my parents with dinner: lemon garlic Parmesan chicken and veggies. As I'm dredging eggy chicken in breadcrumbs, Mom stops chopping potatoes to look over at me. "How was your day, love?"

A simple question, but it still makes me freeze. Her words carry a weight. *How was rehearsal? Are you going to perform well enough to get accepted into Juilliard, blow past the expectations your brothers have already exceeded?* That's what she's really asking.

I focus on the food in front of me so I don't have to meet her eyes. Maybe then I can get my heart to stop beating in my throat. "Fine."

"That's all?" Dad chuckles heartily, rinsing a lemon in the sink.

"Rehearsing went well," I continue, pressing breadcrumbs into another chicken breast. Now even the sound of running water hitting the sink's steel basin is too loud, pressing against my eardrums. "It's nice to play with Daisy."

I feel my parents exchange a look over my shoulders. I've never had a romantic relationship before, so they probably aren't sure how to talk about this with me.

"It seems like you two are getting along well," Mom says.

"Yes." I nod, almost smiling. "She's really good. She makes it feel easy, natural." I look up just in time to watch my dad raise his eyebrows and my mom smile.

"It's not like that," I say quickly.

"We didn't say anything!" Dad laughs and puts his hands up.

I go back to the breadcrumbs, but my face goes warm. She isn't my girlfriend, but something is happening between us. "I think we're becoming real friends."

"That's lovely," Mom says softly.

• • •

"I need your help," Mazhar stage-whispers the next day in the orchestra room.

"Help?" I repeat, my voice at the same volume. "With what?"

"I need to figure out how to ask Amal to the winter semiformal."

Daisy groans between us.

"Seriously?" I feel guilty for being slightly disappointed. "But she's your girlfriend—can't you just invite her?"

"You've got it all wrong. Just because she's my girlfriend

doesn't mean I should expect her to want to come. You have to keep the magic alive," Mazhar says.

"They've been together for *four* years," Daisy adds.

"That just means I need to get more romantic," Mazhar replies, determined. "The deadline for tickets is the Monday after Thanksgiving. I only have two weeks. Give me some ideas."

"But wouldn't it be more romantic if you thought of them yourself?" I smile when Daisy turns to me and mouths, *Thank you.*

"You cellists and your logic," Mazhar mumbles.

"For the record"—Daisy raises her hand—"I agree with him."

"So now my own section is turning against me?" Mazhar throws his head up to the ceiling. "Daisy, how could you?"

Before Daisy can say anything, Ms. Silverstein calls for class to begin, sending those of us who have duets to rehearse out of the room.

Daisy and I walk to the stage, our duet's notes already filling my head. But when we sit down across from each other with music stands between us, she waves her hand.

"Before we jump into rehearsing our duet, I had an idea."

I readjust my glasses, blinking against the lights above our heads. "What is it?"

"What if we blow off rehearsing for a song or two, and just have a little fun?" she says.

"Really?"

"Yeah." Daisy nods. "Let's just play something new and upbeat. Let's just play because we want to, not because we have to practice."

The way she ends her sentence sounds like there's more she wants to say, but instead of pressing her, I run a rosin stick along my bow. "Without sheet music?" I ask instead as she puts her own rosin away.

"You didn't need it when you snagged us that gold at NYSSMA last year," Daisy points out, making me go pink.

I look down the neck of my cello, focusing on the bridge instead of her face. "I practiced that piece for months."

"You always do." I can hear the smile in her voice, and that makes me smile, too.

Resting my cello against my shoulder, I lean forward, assuming first position. "Ready on three."

CHAPTER EIGHT
DAISY

Noah draws his bow across his cello, his fingers gliding up and down the board as he plays. When he begins vibrato, his eyes slide closed, and his thin lashes, framed by tortoiseshell glasses, look like birds behind windows.

The music he's filling this auditorium with—the deep, rich sounds only a cello can produce, played by a person who knows the notes as their own separate language—is the song those birds sing.

He seems different now that he's playing something he's just plucked from his brain. Something fast and bouncy that makes a smile flicker across his face every few seconds.

Noah opens his eyes, not looking at his fingers or his bow. Because he doesn't need to. Instead, he looks at me, his eyes so blue and bright under the lights, and I start playing with him.

CHAPTER NINE
NOAH

Daisy is beautiful.

Performing with her, even when there's no one watching us, is a hell of a time for me to realize that. I've always known she was pretty, but this is different. She's *beautiful*, and I know now, there is a difference between those two words.

Her bow slices through her strings with complete command of her instrument. And as her fingers press down on them, she's smiling. I wonder if it's a conscious thing, or if she doesn't notice at all.

Then her eyes dart from my fingers to my bow to my face, and I know it's on purpose. My stomach flips and at first, I think it's because of the way she is looking at me. But then my chest goes tight.

We're wasting time, my brain suddenly hisses. *Our duet needs to be perfect. It can't be perfect if we keep wasting time.*

My bow clatters to the floor, a pitiful empty echo.

With my cello digging into my shoulder, I bury my head in

my hands. My heartbeat pounds against my eardrums. Lungs suddenly too big for my rib cage are desperate to break it apart. Air tries to claw up the sides of my throat, but it can't find its path along the walls. It keeps slipping down.

I think Daisy is saying my name, asking me a question, but it sounds like I'm underwater, and I can't break the surface.

God, I can't breathe. Why can't I breathe? Why can't I hear anything? Why does my heart hurt from its new place in my ears?

"Noah!" Daisy's voice cracks through my ears. "Are you okay?" Her voice softens. "Do you need me to get the nurse?"

"No." My voice is as thin as a single strand of horsehair on my bow. *She'll just call my parents and they'll start asking questions about why I feel this way and why I haven't told them.* "Pl-please." I pick up my bow. "I'm sorry. I'm okay. This duet, it's—it's just a lot, you know? I let it get to my head."

The bell rings, and I gather myself and walk offstage, rushing to AP Music Theory without Daisy. When she walks in, she glances at me before taking a seat next to Mazhar, and thankfully the teacher quickly jumps into her lesson.

I hide my phone behind my Chromebook and text Daisy.

Noah (2:02 p.m.): I'm not feeling good. Can we skip practice today, please?

Daisy (2:02 p.m.): Sure, no problem. Hope you feel better soon!

After school ends, I slip into the subway, relieved to be just one in a crowd of people I don't know.

"Noah?" Amal waves at me, holding a large clear portfolio case in her hands. A painting of the sunset over the Manhattan skyline—the reds and yellows and pinks falling across silver skyscrapers—stops me in the middle of the train car.

A tourist with a lime-green stroller elbows me out of the way. Amal pats the somehow-empty seat next to her. After maneuvering my cello case around to my front, I sit down.

"That painting is beautiful," I say. "Do you go to that fancy art high school?"

"Dao School for Visual Arts, yeah." Amal beams. "Thanks. I love experimenting with color anywhere I can. Especially in my web comic."

"Congratulations, that school is almost impossible to get into." I hold my cello case closer to me as the train rockets out of the station. "I didn't know you have a web comic."

Amal opens a folder on her phone, showing me art from her comic, *Sunlight Summoner Safa*. Sweeping nighttime landscapes filled with fireflies, characters embracing one another, and even epic battle scenes with magic and swords.

"Wow." I look up at her when she closes her phone. "This is amazing."

"Thanks!" Amal grins, her entire face lighting up. "I just love it so much, and, well, it's important to have fun with our art, right?"

"Sure." I try to smile, but I feel it fade on my face. It's been a long time since music was purely fun for me. I felt it for a minute today, but my anxiety always gets in the way.

"You okay?" Amal asks, furrowing her brow. "You seem kind of bummed."

"I'm all right." Not exactly true, but not a complete lie, either. These attacks only rattle me for a little bit afterward, but I still feel like crap for canceling practice with Daisy.

What does she think about me now? Seeing me like that?

"No," she declares. "You aren't. But we've only just become friends, so I can't wheedle out the truth from you, can I?"

"We're friends now?" My face heats up as I just blurt out the question. I've been electively friendless for as long as I can remember. "I—I mean—"

"You're performing a duet with Daisy," Amal cuts me off. "She's my best friend. And you go school with her and my boy-friend, so we're friends by association." She smiles at me. "If that's cool with you."

"Nice," I find myself saying.

"Perfect." Amal gets to her feet as the train arrives at the Seventy-Second Street subway station. "Mazhar and Daisy are coming over on Friday. How about you come, too?"

"Sure." After I get my cello case back on my shoulders, we shuffle off the train. An East Asian man wearing a tweed blazer and matching flat cap plays the zither nearby, filling the plat-form with shivering notes. "Thank you for inviting me."

Daisy (3:31 p.m.): We don't have to talk about what happened if you don't want to.

Daisy (3:38 p.m.): But I'm here.

Daisy (3:38 p.m.): You know, in case you do.

Noah (4:32 p.m.): The practice room is getting new soundproof panels installed tomorrow. Can we rehearse at your apartment after school instead?

Daisy (4:41 p.m.): Sure.

NOVEMBER 9

Amal (3:58 p.m.): Guess who I sat with on the train?

Mazhar (3:59 p.m.): Who?

Daisy (3:59 p.m.): Who?!

Mazhar (4:00 p.m.): Is it better than that time I sat next to Dolly Parton and was more excited to meet her dog? 🐶

Amal (4:05 p.m.): Close! Noah!

Mazhar (4:05 p.m.): 😮😮😮

Daisy (4:06 p.m.): You haven't said anything about my crush, have you? 😬

Amal (4:07 p.m.): Nope! He's coming over to hang out on Friday. You can confess your feelings yourself then!

CHAPTER TEN
DAISY

My heart has been thrumming in my throat since orchestra. And now that Noah and I are in the lobby of Williamsburg Apartments after an hour of train delays, it feels like it could leap from my body.

I don't know what he's thinking as he gazes from the notice-board to a display of yellow chrysanthemums. *Is he comparing the fluorescent lights above our heads to the warm glow of his lobby? Is he noticing how the windows aren't as shiny?*

Before I open my mouth to ask either of these ridiculous questions, the elevator doors open with a ding. Out walks Mrs. Pecora, an elderly lady who lives on the third floor and attends every single Mass offered at St. Vincent de Paul.

Her brown eyes brighten when she sees me. She tugs her thin bronze glasses down her nose just a little, and the chain they're on slides against her wizened neck.

"Why, hello, Daisy." She speaks slowly to me, like I can't process her speech patterns if she talks normally. Like I'm Holly's age. "How are you today?"

My left arm tightens, curling my hand into a fist that I desperately want to lower, but I can't because of involuntary muscle contractions.

"I—" My voice catches in my throat, making Mrs. Pecora's brow furrow deeper. "I'm well, thank you, Mrs. Pecora."

"Every day is a gift from the Lord!" She beams at me, and I plaster a fake smile on my face. She's an Italian American Roman Catholic grandmother who's from a time even before my own grandparents, who probably prays for everyone on Father Benedetti's list he includes in the programs, who probably prayed for me when everyone at St. Vincent de Paul heard I'd been born early and was diagnosed with cerebral palsy.

My parents were so grateful for their support that they still have the program taped into my baby book, the one that has my name printed on the prayer list in the back.

"Speaking of Him," Mrs. Pecora continues, oblivious, "are you going to tonight's Mass?"

"No." I clear my throat, readjusting my violin case on my shoulder. "No. I have practice."

"Ah." She purses her lips, the same way she does when Mr. Zanetti brings his lemon tarts to fellowship. "Well, prayer can do wondrous things, Daisy, even for the most afflicted. Have a blessed day, now."

"You too."

My reply is too small for her to hear as she shuffles away, content that she has been a Good Catholic today.

Noah and I are quiet until we step into the elevator. I can't even bring myself to look at him, but I hear him drag his fingers through his hair.

"Are you okay?" he asks after the elevator passes the fourth floor.

I'm used to people like Mrs. Pecora, as depressing as that sounds. People have always seen me as someone to be pitied and prayed for, in the hopes that "God will heal me of the condition that I cannot possibly be comfortable with." Except this time Noah saw her, too.

"No," I say, surprising myself, sighing to keep the tears inside. "I'm not. But I am used to it. It's over. Let's just focus on our duet, okay?"

"Sure." Noah rests his left hand over my own, which is still balled up into a fist, but at his touch, it opens involuntarily, wrapping around his pointer finger. Before I can freak out about the fact that we're *actually touching*—or how warm his skin feels against mine—a callus from his cello presses my skin. I have calluses from my violin. Our scars are mirrors, which reminds me that I'm a talented musician, just like him. That I'm more than the person Mrs. Pecora prays for.

"Thank you."

We let go of each other's hands once we reach my floor and

walk to unit C-7. My heartbeat kicks up again as I open the door. I wonder what he'll think of the older couches, the smaller kitchen with appliances that are less shiny than his. How the quilts Nonna Silvia brought over from Italy are the nicest things we own.

"Daisy?"

My mom is standing in front of the mirror near the TV. Her hair is down and wavy. She's wearing a black skirt and an eggplant sweater with matching earrings dangling from her lobes. She doesn't smell like the flower shop, either. Instead, the scent of her strawberry shampoo fills the room.

"Ma?" I stand rooted in the doorway, Noah bumping into me from behind. "What are you doing home?"

"Didn't you get my text?" she asks, tutting when I shake my head. "Nonna and Nonno surprised your dad and me!" She's beaming now, which throws me off a little. My mom is usually too tired for anything more than a small smile. "They got us tickets to see *The Lion King*. Nonna said we needed to get out and do something for ourselves. I can't remember the last time your dad and I had a date, to be honest." She stops, blushing beneath her makeup. "Can you—"

"Watch Holly?" I finish, trying to squash the frustration that courses through my veins. They have time to go see *The Lion King*, but they haven't been to a show of mine in four years? How is that fair? "Sure. She likes music. She can judge our rehearsal."

"Oh." Her eyes go wide. "Daisy, I'm sorry. I forgot you had practice."

"It's okay, Mrs. Abano," Noah says, his voice sending shivers down the back of my neck.

Ma walks over to us, kissing my cheeks, then ducking around me to stretch up and kiss Noah's. She thanks us, then calls for Dad, who lumbers down the hall. He's in a gray blazer that complements her sweater, in addition to his salt-and-pepper beard.

"Sal Abano," he introduces himself as he and Noah shake hands. "There's dinner in the fridge. Leftover pasta fagioli."

"Thanks."

My parents go down the hall to say goodbye to Holly, and Noah and I set up our instruments on the living room couch. I watch him as he takes in the photographs hanging on the walls. My baptism, where I was swallowed by my white gown. Me holding Holly for the first time. Holly with her face covered in lime-green frosting from her smash cake at her first birthday.

"How old is she?" Noah asks.

"Two," I say.

Holly herself comes running into the living room. "Dizzy!" She tackles me around the middle, just as I place my violin on the coffee table.

"Hi, bean." I pull her into my lap, kissing the top of her head.

"We'll be back!" Dad tells us. "Don't stay up too late."

Just as the door closes, Holly climbs from my lap and onto the cushion separating me and Noah.

"Hi," he says, tentative. "I'm Noah. You must be Holly."

"Hi!" My baby sister claps, her pink sweatshirt almost pooling over her pudgy hands. "Yes."

"You know how you love music, Holly?" I ask; I'm convinced there isn't a toddler more in love with the Disney musicals than her. She nods. "Well, can Noah and I play some for you?"

"Peas!"

For the next hour, Noah and I rehearse our duet. Our vibratos bounce around the living room, leaving my baby sister transfixed between us.

"Dizzy?" When we stop playing, Holly points at Noah's cello. "What is?"

"Care to do the honors?" I ask him.

"Sure." Noah leans over and plops Holly onto his lap. "Holly," he begins, unsure about how to explain something to a toddler. "This is called a cello. It's different from Daisy's violin. Would you like to see how?"

Holly nods eagerly, and Noah plays each string once, letting her listen to them. "See? What do you think?"

"Pretty," she declares.

"Thank you." He smiles at her, then at me, just before Holly falls asleep right on his chest.

"Um," he whispers. "Can you . . . ?"

Without him needing to finish that sentence, I carefully put our instruments against the wall.

"What do we do now?" Noah's voice is low. "Should I take her to her room?"

"No," I whisper back. "Holly always wakes up whenever anyone lays her down. She'll be fussy." Mostly, I don't want Noah to know that we share a room. I bet he never had to share with either of his brothers. "If you don't mind just sort of letting her sleep?"

"Sure, no problem." Noah leans against the couch, his back meeting Nonna Silvia's purple quilt. "It'll give me practice."

"Practice?" I repeat, confused, pulling my legs up to my chest. It's getting too cold to rely on dresses and leggings, so today I'm in a pair of dark-wash jeans and a raspberry cowl-necked sweater. Aside from the first pair of jeans I've ever seen him wear, Noah's in a cream sweater over a button-down that's the same color as his eyes.

I'm trying not to concentrate on that last part. Too much.

"My brother Gavin." Cradling Holly to his chest, Noah angles his chin up to the ceiling. And that's when I realize he has a small silver scar there shaped like a crescent moon. "He and his wife, Isla—"

"Isla?" I repeat. "As in, the person who arranged your cello part?"

"Yeah." He nods. "They just had a little girl. They live in Glasgow, so we haven't met her yet. But now, if my niece falls asleep on me, I'll know what to do."

"Oh." My family is as close as it gets; my grandparents literally live right next door. I can't imagine Holly being an ocean apart if she has children one day. "Can I ask you something?"

Noah nods.

I blow out a breath between my teeth. If I don't ask him now, away from the chaos of the concert and the academy, I might never get the nerve to. "Does your family know about what happened to you onstage yesterday?"

Noah's quiet. The only sounds either of us hear are Holly's gentle snoring and Williamsburg outside.

"No." He sighs. "And I don't want to tell them, either."

My mouth falls open. "Why not? They could help you. Wouldn't they want that?"

"I can't let them know I'm not—" Noah murmurs this only to himself, but my heart squeezes all the same. "The rest of my family is so successful. I started playing when I was three, and I debuted at Carnegie Hall when I was eleven. Ever since then I have felt this intense pressure to live up to them."

He debuted *where*?

My heart thuds in my chest. While Noah was learning the cello, I'd just gotten the hang of walking and talking. When he was on one of the biggest stages in the world, I'd had my second leg surgery.

Our lives are even more different than I realized that day at his penthouse. Each of us carrying around our own weight.

"My parents always tell me," Noah continues, "I'm bound

to excel wherever I end up or wherever I play. But that's not enough."

"But your music is enough." Without thinking, I touch the back of his hand, running my finger along his middle knuckle. "*You* are enough. You know that, right?"

"Enough isn't good enough. I want to be greater than they ever imagined. They deserve that from me."

"Why?"

"I don't know . . ." Noah's voice trails off as my fingers fall away from his hand. "Isn't it your dream to go to Juilliard? Same as mine?"

"Yeah," I say quietly, watching his Adam's apple bob up and down. Dreams of performing on grand stages with my violin beneath my chin and gold light at my back. "But that's all it is for me. A dream. I can't afford to go to Juilliard. Even if I get accepted, there aren't enough scholarships and grants to cover my tuition." I have never said this out loud to anyone before, and it leaves a sad taste in my mouth, like swallowing my own tears. "You don't have to wake up from your dream. I eventually do. That's why I have backups. I'll probably wind up going to a community college for a business degree and helping my mom with her flower shop."

Noah readjusts his glasses, his jaw set, with the slightest bit of dark stubble lining his skin. "But you love music, and you are so talented," he murmurs. "Daisy, you can't do that."

"What if I have to?" The question wobbles in my mouth,

like my violin strings when they're out of tune. "What if there's no other choice?"

"We're at the academy for a reason," Noah reminds me. "You should be allowed to pursue your dream."

"Maybe," I whisper. "But you should also be allowed to tell your parents what happened."

Holly sighs in her sleep.

Noah balances her in one arm while reaching his other hand across the couch, threading his fingers with mine. "Maybe," he whispers back.

NOVEMBER 10

Daisy (10:05 p.m.): Are you busy on Thanksgiving? Like, really early in the morning?

Noah (10:10 p.m.): We're going up to Purchase to see my mom's family at noon. But I'm free in the morning. Did you want to practice beforehand?

Daisy (10:12 p.m.): No. My dad is a balloon handler in the Macy's Thanksgiving Day Parade. He gets tickets for 4 bleacher seats. Holly's too little to be up that early, so Mazhar, Amal, and I are going. Wanna come with us?

Noah (10:20 p.m.): Yeah!

Daisy (10:21 p.m.): Awesome! Meet in front of Holy Trinity Lutheran Church at 7 a.m.?

Noah (10:22 p.m.): I'll be there. Thanks for inviting me.

CHAPTER ELEVEN
DAISY

On Thanksgiving, by the time Mazhar, Amal, Noah, and I are settled in our bleacher seats on Central Park West, we're all too excited to pay any attention to how cold, or how tired, we are.

"Have you ever been to the parade before?" Mazhar asks Noah, sipping from his hot chocolate.

Noah thinks for a second. He's wearing a black hat with red lines and a matching puffball, in addition to his usual black pea-coat and tartan scarf. It matches the quilt he brought along with him, which is big enough to cover all our laps.

"Maybe when I was really little," he muses. "I think when my nan and papa were here once."

"They live in Scotland, right?" Amal asks. He nods. "Are they coming in today? Mine flew in from San Francisco." She smiles. "They're staying with my cousin's family. It'll be nice to see them today."

"We fly to Scotland for Christmas and in the summer." Noah takes out his phone. He shows us a picture of a young man who is the spitting image of Noah, except with wire-rimmed glasses and slightly shorter hair, beaming as he gently hugs a beautiful freckled woman. Her brilliant red hair is pulled into a knot at the top of her head, and she's lying in a hospital bed as she holds a tiny baby swaddled in a pink blanket. "That's my brother Gavin and his wife, Isla," he explains. "The morning my niece, Ava, was born."

"She's so cute!" I coo.

"Have you met her yet?" Mazhar asks.

Noah shakes his head. "Not yet, but we will when we fly there next month. Hang on." He swipes the photo away, and instead of another photo, there's a note, written in Mazhar's neat block handwriting:

DEAR AMAL,
I HAD TO DO THIS IN A WAY YOU
WOULDN'T EXPECT. WILL YOU GO TO
THE WINTER SEMIFORMAL WITH ME?
I LOVE YOU,
MAZHAR

I look across from Noah to Mazhar, who's beaming. He figured out a way to ask after all. Then I shift my gaze to Noah. He's smiling, too, almost as widely as Mazhar, and it makes my stomach flip.

"Meri Jaan!" Amal wraps her arms around him. "Of course I will. You didn't have to ask!"

"Yes, I did," Mazhar replies simply.

The parade starts up with a Broadway performance as it always does. I steal a glance at Noah, who's watching the performance with rapt attention.

Then my phone vibrates from my coat pocket and I fish it out. There's a text from Amal:

Amal (9:05 a.m.): I saw you looking! Ask Noah! Before he goes to Purchase!

The words pop against my eyes like camera flashes, even as the floats and balloons pass us by. The crowd—all three and a half million people—are enraptured by the colors, the sheer size of the balloons, the pageantry of it all.

The whole parade passes in a blur because I can't stop thinking about the winter semiformal. I didn't think I even wanted to go—because God knows I can't dance—but now I can't stop imagining Noah and me in matching outfits standing awkwardly against the wall of the gym. *Maybe we could touch hands again?*

"I can't believe you!" Amal whispers as we squeeze our way through the thick sea of people after the parade is over. "You had the entire parade to ask Noah!"

"What am I supposed to say?" I feel my chest getting uncomfortably warm beneath my coat.

Amal gestures forward. Mazhar and Noah are a few people ahead of us, thanks to their longer legs. But because Noah's tall, we can see them easily. I can't figure out what they're talking about, though, not through all the other conversations around us. "Ask him!" she says like it's the easiest, most obvious thing in the world. "You guys have been flirting all morning anyway, so a simple 'Noah, will you go to the winter semiformal with me?' should be enough."

"*Flirting?*" I repeat, my face now as hot as the rest of my body. "That's ridiculous. We haven't been—"

"We don't have time to debate this!" she sings.

I roll my eyes as a blush paints my cheeks. *Sure, Future Mrs. Tilki, romance is so easy. How do I just ask Noah to a dance? Why is this harder than rehearsing our duet? It's just a question!*

Before I know it, the four of us are in front of the 81st Street–Museum of Natural History subway station that will take me back to Brooklyn. They're all waiting for me to say goodbye.

But I'm frozen on the sidewalk.

C'mon, Daisy, I tell myself, squaring my shoulders. *The deadline for tickets is Monday. If you don't ask him now, you can't go to the dance together.*

"Noah?" I step forward just as Mazhar and Amal step back, giving us space. Both of them are behind Noah, with identical smiles.

Noah shifts in his coat, hugging the folded tartan blanket to his chest. He looks confused as a chilly gust of wind blows his brown curls across his face. "Yeah, Daisy?"

"I need you to ask me to the winter semiformal."

We silently stare at each other for a moment.

"Daisy." My name shivers in his mouth, the way his fingers never do against his instrument. "Will you go to the winter semiformal with me?"

My breath catches in my chest anyway. "Yes."

We smile at each other, our cheeks pink as our friends cheer and clap, jumping up and down.

"Thank God." Noah steps closer, pulling me to him, the blanket squashed between us. He wraps his arms around my waist, his touch chasing away the cold. I snuggle into him as he rests his chin on top of my head. He smells warm, like cinnamon. "I've been thinking about asking you all morning."

CHAPTER TWELVE
NOAH

"His tie isn't straight," Gavin says from Douglas's phone.

"Yes, it is." Douglas pulls me over to him for approximately the fifth time in two minutes, balancing his phone against a wooden fruit bowl. Our mugs empty of tea and a plate filled with shortbread crumbs lie next to it. "It's late in Glasgow. Your daughter is making you delirious."

"Here. Let me see." Mazhar turns me toward him, peering at my black tie. He's wearing a white dress shirt, pressed khakis, and bright pink tie that I'm positive has sequins in it. I almost feel underdressed. "Why are you so worried?" he asks. "You're wearing a kilt, which is better than any tie."

"I like you," Douglas says, clapping Mazhar between his shoulders and beaming.

"The original purpose of the kilt was for battle," Gavin chimes in, burping Ava as he speaks. "And in a way, our little brother is entering the battlefield of dating—"

"My tie is fine." I smooth down the Moray clan tartan as my brothers howl. "Guys, they'll be here soon."

It's Friday, the night of the winter semiformal. Mazhar came up to the penthouse to get ready, while Daisy and Amal are doing the same thing right downstairs. Knowing that I'm so close to seeing Daisy dressed up makes my heart sail into my stomach.

And my brothers are "here," too, because they wanted to help me get ready for what they're calling "my first date."

It is. My stomach dips, the hairs on my arms standing up beneath my silk shirt. *It* is *my first date.*

Dad emerges from the bathroom and makes his way over to us, peering at Douglas's phone. "How's my wee granddaughter, eh?"

Gavin goes to laugh, but it fades into a yawn. "Keeping me on my toes."

Dad laughs for him. "That's what she's supposed to do. Don't worry." He looks over at me, rubbing his beard. "Aye, what's this?" He doesn't even wait for us to say anything; he just flips up the collar of my white dress shirt and redoes my tie. "There. Lord knows how the three of you still haven't managed to tie a tie properly."

"I told you!" Gavin hisses. His celebration is cut short when Ava spits up all over her burp cloth. He groans. "Ava, why now, sweet girl? Guys, I should go."

"See you in a few weeks," Dad tells him as Douglas and I wave goodbye. "Call your mum tomorrow."

Gavin clicks out of FaceTime just as Mazhar's phone rings. It's Amal, telling us that she and Daisy are in the lobby.

I convince Dad and Douglas that they don't need to accompany us into the elevator (though they insist on taking pictures). My heart pounds the entire ride down.

But when the doors slide open, I forget why I was so worried. Amal has coordinated Mazhar's tie with her matching sari and gold hijab, and they look happier than I've ever seen either of them. Daisy makes me feel like I'm floating.

She's wearing a long-sleeved navy-blue dress. Her hair is out of its usual braid, cascading down her shoulder in waves I didn't know she had and suddenly feel guilty for not noticing. The top half of the dress gives way to a full skirt that bells out around her, the flower pattern throughout it shimmering beneath the fluorescent light.

I wonder if she's aware of how beautiful she is.

"Hi!" they chorus.

"Hi." I smile at them, and Daisy steps forward. I slip my arm through hers. Shivers race along my skin. And as we walk, I can't stop noticing the rustle of Daisy's skirt against my leg.

"Your dress . . ." My voice trails off. "It's really pretty."

"Thank you. It belonged to Mazhar's older sister, Rabia." She smiles up at me. "Your kilt looks nice on you, too."

I turn as red as the kilt itself, smiling a little bit. "Thanks."

"All right, get together," Mazhar says. "The Morays made me promise I would send them a photo."

· · ·

There is glitter on every possible surface of the gym, and I'm convinced the DJ thinks everyone from here to Long Island needs to be blessed with his curated playlist.

We've been here for over an hour, and I still haven't asked Daisy to dance.

Instead, we've been watching Mazhar and Amal dance with everyone else. Even Beaux is grinding up against a girl from senior band.

I look over at Daisy and find that she's looking at me. Studying me, like I'm a math problem she can't figure out.

"Do you want to dance?" she asks.

Yes, I do.

But instead, I say, "No," and I watch as Daisy's eyes widen, knowing that I have made tonight needlessly confusing for both of us.

"I'll be right back," I mumble. "I just need some air."

I pivot on my heel without exactly waiting for her to reply. But for once, my need to breathe keeps my brain from snagging on to the fact that I was a bit rude.

I'm not giving myself time to think about that.

As my heart pounds in my chest, as my lungs shrink, as my shoes carry me through the gym, down the hall, and out into the courtyard with a skeletal maple tree that bisects the concrete slab, I'm only thinking about Daisy.

She's perfect. Bright and beautiful and complex in the way

her violin is. The ever-present traffic beyond the fence kicks up a gust of the bitter December cold. It gnaws at my fingers, like it knows the most vulnerable part of my body.

The chill keeps me grounded. It's why I came out here.

The door opens, and I skitter closer to the maple, looking over my shoulder. I desperately don't want to be seen right now. I need more time to gather my thoughts.

It's Daisy. She steps closer to me, and I mirror her, as if we rehearsed this. We know the notes; we don't need to look at the sheet music. We know where we're going; we don't need to watch our feet.

"What are you doing out here?" She holds the skirt of her dress in bunches, flowers gathered in her fists. "You'll freeze."

"So will you." I glance at the sheer sleeves, wondering if goose bumps are sprouting up her arms, resisting the urge to reach over and find out.

It's quiet, the only sounds between us the perpetual motion of the city beyond the fence. "Look," Daisy says finally, speaking to the light bouncing off the skyscrapers. "If you came out here because of me, I'm—"

"No." I clear my throat. "I mean, yes."

"Which is it?" She's trying to tease me, but there's a slight tremor at the end of her question. "If you didn't want to dance with me, why did you even ask me to come with you?" Daisy closes her eyes for a second before grabbing the skirt of her dress again. "Did you just ask me out of pity? Because I asked you to?"

My mouth falls open, but the words won't come out.

She shakes her head, taking a step back. "I thought you were different—"

"The reason I haven't asked you to dance is because you look beautiful tonight!" I blurt out. My words ring around us like our instruments echoing off the auditorium walls, and my shoulders crumple inward. "And that makes me nervous! I can't think straight and I'm not sure what to say or do next. I—I was unprepared!"

She stares, her cheeks flushed. "Excuse me?"

"I—I mean." I rake my right hand through my hair, plucking my curls the way I pluck my cello strings. "Ever since that day we were paired up, my brain's divided itself between two things: music and you. Daisy, I don't know what to do with how I feel about you."

"Noah," Daisy whispers. "You like me?"

Yes, I want to say. *I like you.*

"But it doesn't even matter because I can't focus on anything other than our duet," I say instead, dropping my hand. "Our performance is too important."

"I need you to be honest with me." Daisy hugs her arms closer to her chest, her voice as soft as her dress. "Are you okay?"

She tried to talk about this onstage when I had my anxiety attack. Then again in her apartment.

Only, I didn't listen to her and I should have.

"I—" The words fade in my throat on their way up. "Daisy, I don't know. I'm not really sure. Honestly."

She holds out her hand. "Would you like to dance?"

I weave my fingers through hers. Both our hands are freezing, but touching her makes me feel warm.

When we get back to the gym, Daisy just stands next to me like a pillar overlooking a sea of blue and silver glitter, cheesy Top 40 songs being played at an earsplitting volume.

"Are you trying to memorize the beat, too?" Her question throws me; I cock my head to one side like my dog.

I click my tongue, a smile unfurling across my face. "Are you asking me if I can dance?"

"Coordination isn't my thing." Daisy smiles back, but pink splotches across her cheeks. "Making music? That I can do. Moving to it?" She shakes her head. "Nah."

"I could show you if you want," I offer, squaring my shoulders.

We get onto the dance floor, and I pause, unsure for a moment of where to put my hands. But then Daisy's eyes cut to mine again, and my nerves settle. I show her where to put her left hand, on my shoulder. My entire leg trembles at the light pressure.

"Now what?"

"Take my hand."

We both watch as her right hand folds into my left. Her grip is soft—but with calluses dotted along her fingers—and I relax into her.

"Are you sure this is okay?" she asks. "I'll be stepping on your feet soon, too, and I don't want to hurt you."

I shake my head, feeling a few curls fall across my forehead. "You won't hurt me." Positioning my right hand at her underarm, I step back to turn us into a waltz, and she follows me, immediately crushing my left foot beneath hers.

"Noah, oh my God!" She groans, laughing. "I told you, I can't dance. Are you okay?"

"Perfect." I spin her out so she can't see my grimace, bringing her close to me when she twirls back. With me leading, we move across the floor, somehow avoiding colliding with everyone else.

"We're not following the music at all." Her eyes light up like the flowers on her dress. "This song is in a 4/4 time signature."

"And a waltz is in 3/4," I reply, beaming.

Daisy bounces on the balls of her feet. "Let me spin you now."

I blink, readjusting my hand against her back. "But I'm a foot taller than you. How—"

Daisy pulls her left hand from my shoulder, grabbing on to my right hand with her own and twirling me so fast that stars pop against my glasses. I turn back, gazing down at her. Performing at Carnegie Hall doesn't even come *close* to the feeling she gives me. "Like that." She collapses against my shirt as she giggles. I haven't had this much fun in years. "Surprised you, huh?"

Daisy, I want to whisper in her ear as we sway, momentarily oblivious to the rest of the school still around us. *You do way more than surprise me.*

CHAPTER THIRTEEN
DAISY

The night of the holiday concert, I walk into school wearing a white button-down blouse and black skirt. My matching black tights already have a run down the side, and my palsied left foot is slipping around in my Mary Janes the way it always does, no matter how much cotton Ma stuffs into the toes.

"We'll be cheering for you from the audience, sweetheart!" she said as I was walking out the door. By some miracle, my parents managed to get the night off and find a sitter for Holly. As happy as I am that they'll be there, it's also twisted my stomach into knots.

My knuckles are white from gripping the strap of my violin case, and I only drop my hands when I push through the door into the orchestra room. The show doesn't start for another hour, but as usual, performers have arrived early to warm up.

The familiar sound of the instruments calms me, even

though it's all chaos, scales, and people tuning their strings. Ms. Silverstein arranged everyone to sit according to their section, so I take my seat next to Mazhar. He stops rosining his bow to grin at me.

"Hey."

"Hi."

I flip open my case, grabbing my own rosin stick and running it along the length of my bow.

"You're late, Differently Abled," Beaux points out. He's practically leaning across Zachary Ogawa and Jasmine Wright, the third- and fourth-chair violinists, who glare at him. "How can you expect to join a professional orchestra someday if you can't even get to rehearsals on time? They won't make exceptions just because you're cr—"

"Oh, yes." I round on Beaux, jabbing my bow toward his dress shirt, relishing how he missed a few wrinkles. Zachary and Jasmine watch me, beaming. "The city's history of subway delays is my fault."

"Obviously," Mazhar adds.

"Now," I say, moving my bow away, "let me rehearse, please."

"Wait." Beaux rises from his chair, crossing behind our row.

My body stiffens when I feel his long, cold fingers on the back of my shirt collar. My stomach drops to the cotton in my shoes, but I whirl around to face him anyway at the same time as Mazhar.

"Don't touch me," I growl as Mazhar steps between us.

"I was just trying to help," Beaux simpers, leaning against

his seat. "Her collar was rumpled on the left side. She can't reach it herself."

"That doesn't mean you just can adjust it for me," I spit back.

"Forget him," Mazhar says, and we turn to our music stands, tuning out Beaux's mumbling. "Nervous about tonight?"

"No," I lie, stealing a glance across the room. More specifically, at the cello section. Noah must have already gone through his scales, because I recognize his finger movements from our piece. He takes his eyes off his music stand to look at me. He waves with his bow-free hand, and I smile back.

"Sure," Mazhar drawls.

"Rehearse your piece," I mumble, running through my scales to ignore the warmth in my cheeks.

"Don't worry." Mazhar puts his rosin away. "We can all relax tonight." After the show, our teachers are throwing us a party in the auditorium.

For the next hour, we run through warm-ups and practice. After our third run-through, Ms. Silverstein leads us and our instruments out into the hallway, quietly telling us to sit in our section order so that walking onstage will go smoothly.

I balance my violin on my knee with one hand and press my bow frog to my blouse's top button with the other. I feel my heart trying its best to beat out of my chest as I look across the hall to Noah, whose spine is perfect against the back of his folding chair, but whose eyes are gazing into mine.

It's not *performing* that has me nervous. At least not this part. *It's Noah.*

And the fact that, soon, we'll be sitting beneath hot stage lights, performing a piece that everyone in the auditorium will watch and hear.

My muscles don't loosen until after the musical theater section of the concert is over. The theater students file through the backstage, led by Mr. Castillo, who pauses to smile at Ms. Silverstein, both of them blushing to the roots of their dark hair.

"You were all fantastic!" Ms. Silverstein compliments him. "As always."

"Thank you, Rachel." He goes to reach for her but stops himself. Ms. Silverstein returns his smile, her dimples popping.

The rest of us congratulate the musical theater students as they follow him, perhaps overenthusiastically, to distract from the fact that we are now positive that our conductor is dating their director. Noah leans over to me. "We'll be amazing," he whispers, his knuckles white around his own bow frog.

"Of course we will," I whisper back as we settle in to listen to the band next.

• • •

I'm so focused that I startle when Mazhar gets to his feet and nods at Eric, who's sitting next to Noah behind us. "You're up?" I ask him.

Mazhar nods, his Adam's apple bobbing as he swallows. "Yeah. Wish me luck."

"You don't need it," I grin as he starts to walk away.

"I love you, Meri Jaan!" Amal cheers from an unseen part of the auditorium.

Mazhar spins on his heel in a way that makes me envious, cupping his hands around his mouth as best as he can while holding both his violin and bow. "I love you, too, canım!" I just shake my head.

Watching Mazhar play is always a completely surreal experience. Everyone at this school is talented, but Mazhar's love for his instrument goes beyond the mastery that earned him first chair.

"Wow." Noah's whisper in my ear sends shivers stampeding down my spine once Mazhar and Eric are done and the auditorium fills with applause. "They're fantastic."

"I know," I murmur, unable to tear my eyes away.

They bow, walking offstage as the audience claps again. I take a deep breath that fills up my whole chest until it's almost painful. I hear Noah do the same. Neither of us says anything as we climb the short staircase to the stage, arrange our sheet music, and settle into our chairs. The legs scrape on the wood of the stage, and the sound seems louder than any piece performed tonight.

I feel like if I so much as breathe, the audience can hear it.

Noah looks at me. His glasses have slid just a bit down his nose as he rests his cello against his body. I position my violin under my chin and raise it, my right fingers poised on the board as my left hand curls into a fist around my bow frog. And when we nod at each other, we start to play the song his brothers composed.

It begins with Noah plucking his C and G strings, each deep sound reverberating around the auditorium. I come in on my A string when he draws his bow across his instrument, cello and violin both given time to swim through the notes, crafting a story without need for words or pictures. There's a longing, one that's equal parts sorrow and joy, in the music we're creating.

As our duet crescendos in a clash of A string on cello and E string on violin, we stand up from our chairs, no longer needing our sheet music. We transition to a complicated, frenzied vibrato that has our instruments pushing back against each other, my left hand tightening even more around my bow as I move it across my strings.

Noah's not looking at his cello, his bow, or his fingers. He's gazing at me, bathed in the hot, prickly wash of the stage lights.

And then. And then. And then.

Noah smiles, drawing his bow across his strings as his fingers travel along his fingerboard. His grin fills my entire chest with warmth that I know isn't from the lights overhead. And his eyes stay on mine as we play the final, shuddering note, allowing it to ring out around the auditorium.

The crowd erupts in a mix of applause and cheering—the loudest there's been tonight. I hear Mazhar and Eric, even Amal, yelling about how amazing we were. But I'm transfixed by

Noah as he steps toward me, instead of facing the audience to bow.

"Daisy." His voice is hoarse, like a dry bow. I glance down, just for a second, to see that strands of horsehair are dangling from both of our bows, before meeting his eyes again. I don't think I've ever seen them this bright, or him this beautiful, this cellist standing beside me onstage.

Our bows clatter to the floor at the same time I reach for Noah. He cups my face in his hands. Lurching into the music stand, needing to be close and oblivious to the splintering crash it makes joining our bows, our bodies press together, hot from the lights and overwhelmed by what we just accomplished.

We're one breath apart, exactly how we stood on this stage the day we were paired up to perform.

Only this time, we close that infinitesimal space, because I kiss him.

A beat passes, one long enough for a realization to sink its claws into my brain as the silence between us fills my ears. Noah isn't moving. His body is stiff like the cello beside him. *Oh God, what was I—*

But then, Noah kisses me back.

His callused fingers trail along my cheeks; electricity pulses through my skin at each new spot he touches, careful, as if I were his cello's strings. All I can think about is the feel of his lips on mine, our hearts beating in time with each other's to create an entirely new duet. My spastic left hand grips his white dress shirt, bunching the thin cotton between my steel-strength fingers, while my right threatens to snap my violin in half.

Just before we open our eyes to the harsh brightness of the stage and the thunderous applause that could probably be heard from atop the Empire State Building, I realize that Noah tastes like tea, and some kind of butter cookie I can't place.

We break apart, pivoting toward the house. Bowing from our hips, we run offstage and burst into the empty hallway. With our chests heaving and our hands linked, I gaze up at Noah.

I choke out a laugh, and he leans closer, my next few words a whisper against his shirt. "We left our bows onstage."

"Yeah," Noah murmurs, tucking me against the wrinkled cotton, a smile in his voice. "We did."

CHAPTER FOURTEEN
DAISY

The double doors leading backstage burst open, and Mazhar emerges, clutching his violin and both of our bows. "Daisy, Noah!" He smirks. "I came as quickly as I could. Everyone else is out in the lobby. Flowers, hugging, congratulations, the usual."

"My parents should be out there," I say, watching my best friend's eyes grow wide. "Did you see them?"

"No, but come on." He jerks his head down the hall. My stomach tangles itself into knots again. *Did they leave already?* "If you want to blend in, you should probably head out there now. I have to find my family." He looks at Noah. "I only came back here first because first chairs need to look out for each other."

Blood rushes to Noah's cheeks. "Thank you."

"You"—Mazhar spins on his heel—"are welcome. Now let's go."

He leads us into the lobby, which is filled with laughter,

conversation, and most importantly, people. Members of the orchestra are still holding their instruments, so happily chaotic string music fills the area, too. We find Mazhar's family talking to Noah's parents and a guy who can only be his brother Douglas. They have the same face, except Douglas is taller, with a thicker build, broader shoulders, and horn-rimmed glasses.

"Congratulations!" Mazhar's mom, Sabah, coos. She presents him with a bouquet of purple crocuses and me with one of orange gerbera daisies.

Amal tucks herself underneath Mazhar's chin. She fits there like a puzzle piece.

"You really didn't have to do that," I say, smiling down at the flowers. My eyes are glassy. "Thank you."

"You're welcome," Sabah murmurs, giving me a strong hug. She steps back, her face glowing along with her silver hijab, and turns to Noah. "You must be Noah," she says. "It's so nice to meet you. You played very well."

Noah shakes her hand. "Thank you, Mrs. . . ." His voice trails off and he goes red again.

"Tilki," she supplies gently.

"She's right, you know." Noah's dad sweeps his son into a tight embrace that crushes him to his ribs.

"That was your best performance yet," his mom adds, giving him a bouquet of sunflowers when his dad releases him. She hands me one of my own, too, and now we're both holding mounds of brilliant flowers.

I try to ignore the small pricking sensation of tears behind my eyes.

"You're an excellent violinist, Daisy." Douglas beams at me. The cellophane of my two bouquets scrunches as he shakes my hand. "I know one when I hear one."

"Thank you." I smile back at him, warmth coursing through my chest at his praise. "And thank you and Gavin for composing that piece for us."

"You're welcome." Douglas adjusts his glasses. "We made a video of it, too. Our subscribers are enjoying it as well. Two hundred thousand views since we uploaded it."

"Wow," I say, my eyes wide. "The school always posts the performances on YouTube. I doubt we'll get half as many views as yours."

"Attention, students!" Mr. Castillo's voice booms across the lobby. "Our after-party is now beginning!"

The families say goodbye, and as everyone else streams into the auditorium, still clutching their instruments, Noah turns to me. "Do you want to join everyone else?" His voice, soft and yet so loud at the same time, floats into my ears, making the hairs on the back of my neck stand up.

I shake my head. My heart pounds against my ribs. "Not yet. Let's go somewhere."

How we manage to run into the orchestra storage room while holding our instruments and bouquets is a feat I'll never understand.

After gently positioning our instruments against the wall and our flowers in an empty cubby, I pull Noah to me. He gazes into my eyes. I nod before he scoops me up into his arms again, crushing us both to the cubbies as he kisses me this time. Noah's lips are somehow more like fire now, away from the stage rather than beneath its lights, as I thread my fingers through his hair. My spastic fingers tug on the strands, and I'm about to figure out how to apologize for involuntary muscle contractions when a sound as low as the C string on his cello escapes from Noah's throat.

"Daisy." His breath shivers against the shell of my ear, his fingers pressing into my wrinkled shirt. Before I can say anything, the door opens again, and Noah lowers me to my feet. A coldness seeps down the back of my blouse.

I look toward the doorway, bright fluorescent light pouring in from the orchestra room making me squint.

"Beaux?" My voice is hard, and his lips quirk into a tight smirk. "What are you doing here?"

"I'm just putting my violin away," Beaux replies simply, holding up his instrument. "And I didn't see either of you in the auditorium. I wanted to see if you were okay." He moves past us and goes to pick up my violin. "I'll put your violin away—"

"Don't—" Noah begins at the same time as I charge between Beaux and my instrument.

"I'll take care of it myself," I mutter, picking it up before Beaux can wrap his fingers around it.

"C'mon, Daisy." Noah gathers up our flowers and takes my hand in his. "Let's get out of here."

Before we walk out into the hallway, I grab my backpack from my seat. When we emerge from the orchestra room, Beaux flits directly in front of us, walking backward toward the lobby. "What's going on between you two?" he asks. "Is Noah your boyfriend now? Differently Abled, how does it feel for someone to finally love—"

"Beaux!" I snap. "Can you please leave us alone?"

"Fine." Beaux snorts. "I was just making conversation."

Noah speeds us up so that we pass him into the auditorium and over to Mazhar and Amal. Luckily, they're in one of the center rows, making it harder for Beaux to spot us. Up in front of the stage, Ms. Silverstein and Mr. Castillo are seated at the piano together. Mr. Castillo's fingers fly across the keys as Ms. Silverstein treats everyone to a flawless performance of "On My Own" from *Les Misérables*, not needing a mic to be heard.

"What next?" Ms. Silverstein asks the front row, laughing. Mr. Castillo scoots a little closer to her, and they share a quiet smile.

"So." Amal grins at us. "What were you two up to just now, hm?"

"Nothing," Noah and I splutter in unison.

Mazhar compliments us on our performance, but I don't hear him. I root through my backpack until I find my phone instead.

Ma (8:45 p.m.): We are so proud of you, Daisy! But we need to get back home to relieve Mrs. Valentini. Ti voglio bene!

She doesn't even say anything about me kissing Noah in front of an auditorium filled with people. You'd think she would, but nothing. I sigh, angling my head up to the ceiling. *Did she even see it, or did they leave before we ever took the stage?*

"Is something wrong, Daisy?" Mazhar asks.

"No." That's a lie, and Mazhar knows it. Noah squeezes my hand, and I look up at him. "It's just . . . my parents." I wipe a few small tears away with my wrist. "They were here. They saw us. I just wish they would have stayed long enough to see us after. I've wanted this for so long, but I guess I should be grateful they finally showed up at all?"

"You can be upset," Noah murmurs. "We worked hard for this."

I sigh again. "But I don't want this to screw up our night. Okay?"

"Okay." Noah kisses the back of my hand without meeting my eyes.

"What about you, is something on your mind?" I ask. "You can tell me. I just told you what I was upset about."

He takes both of my hands in his. "I have a question."

"Sure." I feel my cheeks turn pink. "What is it?"

"Will you . . ." He glances down at our hands, then meets my gaze. "Daisy, will you be my girlfriend?"

"Absolutely." I smile, and he gives me a quick kiss.

"That's so cute I can barely contain myself!" Mazhar whoops gleefully as Amal claps her hands. "Should we go get some food? Orange soda after a show just hits different, you know?"

He's right, and I nod, beaming. But Noah's voice roots me to my chair.

"Um." Noah looks at Amal and Mazhar, then at me, the word wobbling in his mouth. "Actually, can I talk to you guys?"

"Is something wrong?" Amal asks, her brow furrowed.

"I . . ." Noah's voice trails off as he blinks several times. "I don't know."

"Talk to us," Mazhar encourages him gently.

For almost a full minute, the auditorium is our only sound: piano, singing, laughing, drinks being poured. Everyone is too busy celebrating our successful night to pay attention to us.

"So, what's up?" Amal asks finally. Her gold hijab shimmers beneath the lights.

With his fingers shaking, Noah takes his phone from his back pocket. He opens up Safari and types in two words: *anxiety attack*.

The search engine loads in a second, spewing information about panic attacks, anxiety attacks, symptoms, and causes. And with his fingers still shivering against his blue phone case, he shows it to us.

We take a second to read the page.

I meet his eyes first, squeezing his hand. I don't say anything, waiting to see if Noah's going to speak first. But he doesn't. He squeezes my hand again instead. The fingernails on my left hand dig in the slightest bit.

I hope I'm not hurting him.

"You know . . ." Mazhar leans back, making his blue plush seat creak. "When my psychiatrist evaluated me, it wasn't just for depression. They asked me questions about anxiety, too."

Amal's brow wrinkles, but she stays where she is, despite leaning the tiniest bit forward. She blows a breath out from between her lips. "Do you feel anxious right now?" she murmurs.

"No. Yes." The words tumble from his mouth, each of them tripping over the other. "I feel a little bit anxious all the time. Even when nothing is going on, it's there, buzzing just underneath my skin. And I don't know what to do."

"You can talk to your parents," I remind him. "What's standing in the way of that, exactly?"

"A lot," Noah replies simply, getting to his feet. His hand slips out of mine to jam itself into his hair. He blows out a slow breath. "But I'm going to. Now. I'm sorry, but I—I have to go." He closes his eyes and sidesteps out of the row, walking up the aisle.

I stare after him. Mazhar and Amal tell me to make sure

he's okay, and I spill out into the hallway right behind Noah.

"Text me," I murmur as we walk beside each other. "When you're done talking to them. No matter how long the conversation is, no matter how late it is. Okay?"

He kisses me, just once. "Okay."

CHAPTER FIFTEEN
NOAH

I fumble with my key before giving up on trying to get it in the lock and knocking on the door.

"Hello?" Dad's voice makes me jump. I've been so lost in my own mind that I didn't hear his footsteps. "Who is it?"

"Dad, it's me." My voice cracks on the word *me*. Then I remember that he has three sons. "Noah," I add.

He opens the door, wearing plaid pajama bottoms, a gray T-shirt, and actual bunny slippers. The sounds of *Nailed It!* drift down the hallway from the living room. "Did you forget your key?" His voice has the same cadence now as it does when he tells stories about mythical Scottish beasts.

I shake my head. My hands are shivering. Dad steps back so I can get through the door and instead of leading the way, he wraps his arm around my shoulders. We make our way down the hall into the living room. Dad sits on the couch, pausing the show, and pats the middle cushion.

"Did something happen?" he asks. "Your mum and I weren't expecting you back so soon."

It's the same cushion Douglas sat on when he told us he was gay. The same cushion Gavin sat on when he revealed he'd be moving across the Atlantic and away from us. Sitting on it now, between my parents, I have no idea how to explain what's going on in my head.

I've spent so much time pretending it wasn't a problem, I never found the right words.

"Hi, love." Mom kisses my forehead. "You're shaking. What's wrong?" She peers up at my dad. "Is he okay, Lewis?"

"Stay here." Dad touches my knee as if he's afraid I'll leave. "I'll make you a cuppa."

"Red mugs." The simple words scratch at the walls of my throat.

Dad gets to his feet and disappears into the kitchen. Haggis stirs from his plush dog bed in the corner of the living room, stretching his tiny legs and yawning. "Hi, buddy." I drum my fingers on my knees.

My dog trots over, flopping across my feet and looking up at me with his eyebrows raised as if asking, *Well? Why aren't you petting me yet? I've walked all this way.*

Dad comes back into the living room as Mom pushes my hair away to feel my forehead. "Noah, what's going on?" She tuts. "You don't have a fever."

"Dad, Mom." My voice sounds so far away, as if I'm on the street fifty-seven floors below us. "What if . . ." I go to take a breath, but it's like I'm inhaling glass shards instead of oxygen. "I'm sorry."

"Don't apologize." Dad places his mug on the glass coffee table in front of us.

"Take your time," Mom encourages me.

"Okay." I exhale, and this one is slightly easier, even though my fingers are shaking against my mug. "What if I don't get into Juilliard?"

My parents don't speak. They glance at each other, confused, as if they never imagined I might not get accepted. Their faces make my stomach drop.

"Noah," Mom begins. "That doesn't matter to us."

"Not at all," Dad adds. "Wherever you get accepted—"

"I need help," I continue quickly, as if neither of them said anything. "I've needed it for a long time, but I thought if I practiced as much as I could, if I was the best cellist at my academy, if I surpassed everyone else in—in skill and technique and performance, that my mind would—that *I* would eventually be okay."

Leaning forward, I place my mug next to my dad's. "But I'm not." My voice breaks on the last word, and I bury my face in my hands. I'm quiet for a second, long enough to feel my parents turn in their seats next to me, before sobs push my body forward and I nearly fall into the coffee table, stopping myself with my elbows. "And I'm *so* sorry. I shouldn't be like this. It's—it's not what I worked for."

"Noah," Dad whispers, coaxing me back to the couch. "Come, now. Why didn't you tell us you were feeling this way?"

"I didn't know how." My throat clogs up, salt from the tears stinging my eyes. "I—I just didn't want to hurt anyone."

"Oh, Noah," Mom croons, her voice wet. "You could *never* hurt us. Juilliard or not, we just want you to be happy."

Dad pulls me to his side. I cling to him like I'm three years old, afraid that if I let go, I'll cry even harder. Thoughts tumble around in my brain, gathering speed. *What are they thinking? Are they surprised about what I just told them or did they, on some level, expect this sort of thing to happen with me? I bet neither Douglas nor Gavin cried on the couch like this. Why me and not them? What if my parents don't know how to help me?*

"We'll get you the help you need." Mom's words let me climb out of my own head for a second. She stops running her fingers through my hair and kisses the top of my head. "We can start looking tomorrow."

"Thank you." I straighten my spine, swiping my arm across my face.

Mom presses my mug back into my hands, kissing my forehead. "Now finish your tea," she murmurs.

"Want to see some gran ruin a cake?" Dad asks, gesturing to the TV as he retrieves his own mug.

I take a sip of tea, letting its warmth reach my fingertips. "Yes, please."

•   •   •

Later that night, I'm staring up at the ceiling, trying to fall asleep. I kick off my covers and scoot to the edge of the bed. I'm not wearing my glasses, so everything in front of me is fuzzy, even in the dark.

Haggis chose to sleep in my room tonight, but even he stays quiet. The tags of his collar clink together as he raises his head.

I hear the low rumble of my dad's voice, and I get up from my bed, padding down the hallway, even though I know I shouldn't. I should be sleeping, not crouching in the staircase peeking at the floor below.

My parents are standing in front of their wedding picture: Dad in his kilt, Mom in Grandma Fiona's dress standing on the steps of New York City Hall.

The glass railing is slick under my fingers as I clutch it.

"What happened?" Dad mutters. "How did we miss this? Noah's the best musician out of all of us. You've heard him play."

My stomach dips, and I almost lose my grip on the railing. *How?* my brain whispers. *How can they think I'm the best?*

"*Of course* he'd feel pressured," Mom hisses back. "We obviously missed—" The last few words get wet and clogged in her throat. "What if something happened to our son all because *we* didn't notice he was struggling? Did we push him too hard?"

A heavy silence passes between them, horror stories unspooling the longer they go without talking.

"This is my fault," Mom murmurs faintly. "I'm Noah's mother. I carried him for nine months, played my viola for him the day the doctor told me he could hear us, spent nineteen hours birthing him. And I *didn't catch* this."

"Mackenzie." Dad's voice is gruff with his own tears. I grip the railing hard with both hands. He never cries. "Don't you dare blame yourself for this."

"What am I supposed to do?" Mom buries her head in her hands. "Lewis, if we lost Noah because of—"

"But we didn't." Dad cuts her off by folding her hands into his. "Guilt won't get us anywhere."

"I know," Mom murmurs.

This is all my fault. They're blaming themselves because I couldn't keep it together, my brain hisses.

"We can't change the things that led us here," Dad continues. "But we can help him now." He closes his eyes. "I think we should stay here for Christmas. We can still visit Scotland in the summer." As much as I want to go down into the living room, I restrain myself, my toes pushing on the step. "We can see your family this year instead. It probably won't do Noah any good to travel right now."

"We're going." Mom picks up his massive hand, pressing a kiss to his wedding ring. "We're getting Noah help. He's going to be . . ." She sighs, and I can tell she's holding back more tears.

I'm going to be what? my brain whispers. *Okay? How could they possibly know that?*

I slip upstairs and into my room. Closing the door as quietly as possible, I walk back over to my bed and curl up underneath the covers. A few minutes later, I hear my parents climb the stairs and walk past my room to theirs, the floor creaking beneath their footsteps.

Turning my body away from the window, I see the muddled outline of my phone on the edge of my nightstand. The screen lights up with a notification. I hold it close to my face to read what's on-screen.

Daisy (1:06 a.m.): It's late, but I wanted to make sure everything was okay. Even if it's not, I'm here.

My throat tightens as I unlock the phone, navigating to her message.

Noah (1:07 a.m.): Can I call you?

Daisy answers by calling me instead. I pick up immediately, as if my parents can hear my phone vibrating. "Hi," I whisper.

"Hi," she greets me softly. We're quiet for a few beats. "Sorry I'm whispering. Holly had a nightmare, and I just got her back to sleep. How'd it go?"

I tell her everything, like it was some huge epic tale and not a conversation on my living room couch. "None of my other brothers have ever gone to therapy before, so I don't think my parents were prepared for this."

"Your parents love you," Daisy reminds me. "They love you so much, and they just want to help you."

Suddenly I realize how exhausted I am. Thoughts are still churning in my head. It's taken a lot out of me to talk about this tonight. But it feels so much better than pretending to deal with it on my own for years. Before Daisy, Mazhar, and Amal. "I know they do," I say finally. "They're going to start looking tomorrow."

"I'm proud of you." I lean into the phone at her words.

"Thank you."

We don't hang up. Instead, we fall asleep listening to each other's breathing.

And maybe it's just the rush of everything that's happened tonight, but it's the sweetest melody I've ever heard.

The Moray Stage (@MorayStageDG):
We're so proud of our brother and Daisy! Watch them kill this performance! —Gavin

The Moray Stage (@MorayStageDG):
Let's add: We composed this song for them, too! With the help of your wife! Did you forget that part? —Douglas

The Moray Stage (@MorayStageDG):
I love you, @IslaMoray! —Gavin

Isla Moray (@IslaMoray):
I love you, too!

Vivian Wade (@Viviola):
@MorayStageDG Collab when?

Aubrey Abbadelli (@BroadwayQueen117):
#MAMP alumni! Have y'all seen this duet from the winter holiday concert?

CHAPTER SIXTEEN
NOAH

I put my parents in touch with Mazhar's. They were able to get me an appointment with Dr. Singh after school the following Tuesday.

I walk into a sizable waiting room with butter-yellow walls and a large canvas painting of colorful tropical birds that my parents sit underneath after checking me in. I sit across from them, gripping the padded arms of my chair until my knuckles match the snow outside.

Dad walks over to me, Mom's purse in hand. "Before you go in." He unsnaps the main pouch. "These were in our mailbox this morning." He gives me three handmade cards.

The first one is on pink paper, a message from Daisy wishing me luck and telling me to call her after the appointment. She even doodled a small image of me with my cello, with little speech bubbles saying: *Do your best, Noah!*

The second one is on blue paper, Mazhar reminding me that I'm seeing Dr. Singh so that he can help me, that if I need to talk to him about my session, I can.

And the last one I know is from Amal, just by the thick strokes and intricate details of her anime-inspired art style. She's drawn me as a superhero, dressed in blue, punching something unseen off the page. I open the card and see that it's a swirling mass she labeled *anxiety*, and written below that:

You can do this.
Love,
Amal

I pretend I need to hold the card closer to my glasses to shield my eyes, dropping my hands immediately when a door opens.

Dr. Singh exits a hallway, wearing khakis and a dark blue button-down that's the same shade as his turban.

"Noah?" He smiles at me and I nod, shaking his hand. "Hi, I'm Dr. Singh. It's nice to meet you. Come in."

"Your mum and I will be right out here when you're done," Dad tells me as I get to my feet. "Promise."

"Unless you'd like them to come with you," Dr. Singh chimes in. "I let the patient choose, whichever makes them the most comfortable."

"No." The word unsticks itself from my throat. "I'll be okay."

I'm not sure who I'm lying to, or why, but I follow him down a carpeted hallway into a light gray corner office. His diplomas are hung on the wall; a basket of toys ranging from Slinkys to building blocks rests on a table that divides a darker gray sofa and a matching armchair. A modern black desk stretches the length of floor-to-ceiling windows that give way to a view of Central Park. The trees are clusters of bare branches reaching for the skyscrapers.

But even a nice view can't stop the blood from pounding in my ears.

"Let's begin, Noah," Dr. Singh says kindly.

"Sorry." I cough into my elbow. "It's just that I've never done this before."

"Seen a psychiatrist?" I nod, and he writes something down on the tablet that he's balanced on his lap. "Everyone has to start somewhere. Now, I usually get to know a patient by asking them about themselves first. So why don't you tell me about yourself?"

"Well, um. My dad came to the States to play cello in the New York Philharmonic; he was born in Portree, on the Isle of Skye. My mom's a violist in the orchestra, that's how they met. My brother Gavin moved overseas because he got accepted to the Royal Conservatoire of Scotland. Now he plays for the Royal Scottish National Orchestra."

I stop, but Dr. Singh just waves his hand. "There's more you want to say. Go on."

"My parents raised three talented sons and each one of us surpassed the other. I learned the cello three years before either of them even touched their first violin and viola. Even after debuting at Carnegie Hall before my voice started changing, I didn't question my love of music, or my innate ability to play it."

"Because it was expected of you?" Dr. Singh suggests, his stylus positioned above his tablet. I nod. "Your circumstances and talent are both extraordinary. I saw the recent video of your performance." I shouldn't be surprised he watched it, but I am. "Both you and your duet partner—"

"Daisy," I murmur, smiling the tiniest bit.

"Daisy, yes." Dr. Singh nods. "Both of you were brilliant. But do you *enjoy* playing music, still?"

I freeze, unable to even comprehend a life where I never pick up my bow again. "Yeah. But I don't know what to do. This anxiety?" I pause. "This tightness in my chest, my loud heartbeat, the hard time breathing, the racing thoughts, this need to be perfect. It's there. All the time."

Dr. Singh nods, writing on his tablet. "That would be difficult for anyone, especially someone in a family filled with impressive people." He looks up. "How long have these symptoms been happening?"

"Since I was eleven." I sink against the back of the couch, a realization crashing into me. "I had my first anxiety attack then. In the bathroom at Carnegie Hall."

My skill was beyond comprehension for someone so young.

But also, given who my parents were, given how everyone in classical music knew Lewis and Mackenzie Moray, it wasn't that surprising.

Still, somehow, I didn't feel like I was enough.

Before I went onstage, I found myself in the bathroom stall. My hands pressed my glasses to my face. My ribs were too small for my lungs. I gasped for the air I couldn't seem to find. My heart pounded in my throat. The pressure choked me as the beat raced in my ears.

I can see it clearly when I close my eyes. As if that little gangly boy is someone else, desperate for help but too terrified to ask for it.

Like he isn't who I grew up to be.

"I see," Dr. Singh says. "And what is it that you hope to get out of our sessions together?"

"Can you help me?" I open my eyes. "Managing my anxiety, I mean. That is what I have, right?" My cheeks go warm, embarrassed that I've just barely put a word to my feelings after having them for so long.

"After what you've told me today," Dr. Singh begins. I glance at the clock on the wall and realize I've been here for nearly an hour already. "I would diagnose you with generalized anxiety disorder, yes." He taps on his tablet. "I'm going to send you home with some medication. It's important to remember this may not be the one that works for you," Dr. Singh continues. "Treating anxiety disorders varies from person to person, so we could very well have to try something different down the line as part of your treatment plan. I'll send this off to the pharmacy your parents put on your intake form. You'll be able to pick it up today. We can meet again when you get back from Scotland."

"So, if this doesn't work, I will just keep feeling this way?" I can feel the panic rising in my throat.

"Only until we find the right combination of things that do," Dr. Singh replies.

"How long will that be?"

"Noah," he says kindly, leaning forward. "You're here. This is the first step. Let's try and take this one day at a time."

"Thank you, Dr. Singh." I take a deep breath and get up from the couch as he rises from his armchair.

He leads me back out into the waiting room, where my parents are huddled together, each wearing one earbud, watching something on my dad's phone. When they see us, they stand, still stuck together, hurrying to pull the headphones out.

"How'd it go?" Mom asks. Her dark brown hair is frizzy, the way it always gets when she's nervous. Which isn't often.

"Good," I say. "Okay. Fine." Dr. Singh takes them into the hallway to talk, and I grab my phone from my coat pocket and call Daisy.

"Hello?" Daisy picks up on the first ring. "How did it go? How do you feel?"

"Hi." I lean against the wall, next to a painting of a tropical beach. I blow a lock of curls off my glasses. "I'm not sure."

"Do you need me?" She pauses, her words hanging on the line between us. "I mean, do you need *something*?" *Yes*, I want to say. *I need you.* "Do you want to meet up? I can come by."

"Could you?" I blow out a stream of air, but my lungs are still weighed down. "Just tell me where you are. I'll come to you."

CHAPTER SEVENTEEN
DAISY

The old wood floor of St. Peregrine's creaks beneath my snow boots and the wheels of the tiered metal cart from Ma's shop. She put me on delivery duty to the surrounding churches that ordered from us.

Not too far away from the restrooms, Father Holt is chatting animatedly with some parishioners.

"Have a blessed evening, Daisy." He turns to me and smiles.

"Thank you, Father." I grin back at him. "You too."

I've often wished this was my family's congregation because of all the priests I've delivered poinsettias to this afternoon, I like Father Holt the most. He's a wheelchair user, so he understands. He doesn't look at me like I'm in need of healing prayers. Which is ironic, since his church's namesake, Saint Peregrine Laziosi, is one of the patron saints of healing.

It's nice not to be pitied. Father Holt knows that I don't need to be fixed, and I'm not an inspiration by virtue of my existence.

The church doors open, and Noah steps through them, wet, slushy snowflakes clinging to his dark hair. A storm must've just started up outside. It's sticking to the stained-glass windows, clouding up the blues, yellows, and reds.

"Daisy." My name issues from his mouth in a delicious fog that makes my toes curl. "Hello." He takes care to shut the heavy oak doors as quietly as he can. "Is there anything I need to do?" he whispers. "After entering a Catholic church?"

I shift my weight from one foot to the other, hurting from my deliveries. "Are you Catholic?"

"In name only." He shrugs.

Abandoning the poinsettia cart and walking over to him, I take his icy hands in mine, and Noah tucks me into his chest.

"Then you don't need to do anything," Father Holt assures him, coming over to us. He offers Noah his hand. "Caleb Holt," he introduces himself. "I'm the priest of St. Peregrine's."

Noah shakes his hand. "I'm Noah," he says. "It's nice to meet you, Father."

"I need to go find a place for these lovely poinsettias." Father Holt holds up his arrangements. "Tell your mother thank you for me, Daisy."

"I will."

"God bless you both. Merry Christmas," Father Holt adds before disappearing through the doors of the sanctuary.

"How was it?" I ask after the doors shut.

"Weird." Noah's voice is a deep thrum in my ear. "I know things won't get better immediately, but I never talked about my anxiety with a professional. Or anyone, really. Up until now. Dr. Singh prescribed me some medication. He's nice and all, but it's a lot."

"I know." I squeeze his hand, not daring to kiss him in a church. "We need a distraction. Let's go to the park."

We let go of each other. I grab the poinsettia cart, and we head out into Central Park. Snowflakes swirl around us in a mess that, since the holidays haven't come and gone yet, people are still delighted by. We hurry past snow-covered green benches, dodging kids dressed in puffy coats who've scraped together mushy handfuls of it and have started a snowball fight in the middle of the path.

"You would think people have never seen snow before." Noah chuckles, and warmth spreads from my chest to my fingertips.

"It's New York." I smile. "People come here from all over the world to see a train station."

"It *is* a nice train station, though." Noah glances over at me, his eyebrows raised above his glasses.

I laugh as we reach a break in the fence, an entryway to the lawn. "Here seems like a good spot."

"For what?" Noah waits until I get the poinsettia cart onto the grass. I avoid his eyes as the cold causes a muscle spasm to trickle down my arm, choosing to throw myself into the snow.

"This!" I say simply, and begin to make a snow angel.

Noah dives to the ground next to me, face-first, and rolls over onto his back, crafting one of his own. He laughs after a moment, and I realize just how much I enjoy that sound. It's better than any piece of music. I'm glad we're both staring up at the skyscrapers reaching into the white sky, so he doesn't see the blush on my cheeks. "I don't think there's enough snow on the ground to make proper angels," he says.

He's right. I can feel the wet frozen grass pressing against my jeans and my coat, but I don't care. My laughter matches his, the two of us harmonizing.

When Noah turns his head, I can see his cheeks are pink from laughing, his hair dripping, snowflakes clinging to his glasses.

I reach across the snow, knitting our hands together. His calluses press against mine.

"You leave for Scotland soon, right?" I ask.

"Tomorrow," Noah murmurs. "But I'll be back on January second."

"I'll miss you."

"I'll miss you, too."

He leans over, covering my lips with his as his arms find my waist. We kiss, not caring about the snow falling around us or the slush caking our coats.

Noah (4:00 a.m.): I'm here! Did you see the picture of my niece?

Daisy (7:00 a.m.): She's so cute!!!

Daisy (7:01 a.m.): And wow, Gavin has a lot of tattoos.

Noah (7:03 a.m.): Yeah, he has 8. Says he's a glutton for punishment. Which explains the tattoos and, you know, moving an ocean away from us.

Daisy (7:04 a.m.): Aw, stop it. I'm sure he's happy you're visiting.

Noah (7:05 a.m.): He is! He knocked the wind out of me hugging me at the airport. Dad's always happy to come back home, too.

Noah (7:06 a.m.): I'm excited to be here, but I miss you. Is that corny to say?

Daisy (7:07 a.m.): Nope. Because I miss you, too. But don't you dare let it stop you from having fun there, you hear me?

Noah (7:30 a.m.): I showed my gran our performance and she made me teach her how to forward it in an email ☺. She says she likes you and wants you to come visit in the summer.

Daisy (7:33 a.m.): Come with you to Scotland?

Noah (7:35 a.m.): Yeah, what do you say? I apologize for the midgies in advance.

Daisy (7:37 a.m.): I would like that very much.

CHAPTER EIGHTEEN
DAISY

Ma pulls me to the side before we even reach the holy water font inside St. Vincent de Paul, letting the Bellinis pass us instead. It's Christmas Eve, and the wind is whipping around our shoulders in the night.

"Ma, is everything okay?" I wrap my arms around myself once we're on the steps, my eyes watering in the blowing wind. Even my peacoat and woolen dress aren't enough to keep me warm. "It's freezing. We have to go inside." I've been going to church for my entire life, and I'm still not used to bundling up on Christmas Eve to attend midnight Mass. I feel like I should be in bed instead, waiting until Holly wakes up at five a.m., shrieking about the presents Santa left.

"Here." She pulls her thick peacock-patterned cape from around her shoulders and wraps it around mine instead, holding it closed. "So, how are things with Noah?"

"What?" I blink at her. "You couldn't have asked me *inside*? Where it's warm?"

Ma's eyes widen, her voice dropping to a whisper. "Daisy, I can't ask you about a *boy*"—she makes the sign of the cross and I copy her out of habit—"in *church*, on the night before the birth of our Lord and Savior."

"So, we're out on the steps instead?"

"It's the city." She tugs on the tassels of her cape. "It's too loud for God to hear if there's traffic."

"That's not how—" I shake my head. "It's nearly midnight."

"All the more reason to make this quick," Ma quips.

"Daisy!" Mrs. Zanetti, another old church lady, coos as she slowly makes her way up the steps. "My grandson showed me your performance on the YouTube. It was so inspirational! Ottavia," she says, grinning at my mom. "You should be very proud."

I smile at her and say thank you because it's easier than explaining why what she said is wrong. Ma assures Mrs. Zanetti that she is indeed proud before turning back to me.

"You know I hate when they say that." I roll my eyes.

"I know, but she was just being nice. People have been asking about Noah," she continues, changing the subject quickly. "I have to tell them *something*."

I whisper a curse under my breath.

"Daisy Silvia Abano!" Ma gasps. "We are in a church!"

"Actually, we aren't!" I retort back in a whisper. "You

brought us *outside* to ask me about my boyfriend, so we aren't *inside*!"

"Only because you haven't told us anything!" Ma closes her eyes and breathes slowly before opening them.

"Well, you've never asked until now!" I snap, watching as her eyes go wide.

It's not like I've made it easy for her, though. In the days since the concert I've hung out with Mazhar and Amal more than I've been at home. Partly because it's the holiday break, which means Mazhar and I aren't bogged down with the concert anymore. But also to avoid questions about what happened.

Specifically, about the kiss.

The one that, for the last few nights, I've replayed along with each of our other kisses in my head, pretending that Noah is lying in bed with me. Even though he's an ocean away, I can still remember the heat of his mouth on mine.

Mr. and Mrs. Valentini amble up the icy stairs, each of them gripping their grandson's arms for support.

"Merry Christmas!" I say cheerily, hoping it distracts my mom.

"You too, Daisy." The Valentinis smile at us. "God bless."

After they disappear, Ma turns back to me. "Well?"

"We're dating." I pry her cape out of her grip and follow the Valentinis inside, up to the holy water font. "And no," I hiss before she can ask, "we haven't *done* anything."

Ma just sighs, both of us dipping our fingers into the basin and making the sign of the cross again, before taking our seats in a pew at the very back. We always sit here so I don't have long to walk when Mass ends. The kneeling and rising and receiving communion are enough for my legs.

"Dizzy!" Holly's whisper echoes around the church as she reaches her chubby arms out to me once I unbutton my coat and lay it on the pew. I take her from Dad, plopping her into my lap, taking the program he holds out to me.

"Shh." I bounce her up and down, kissing the top of her head. "Remember, we have to be quiet in church. Okay?"

"Jesus birday," Holly murmurs almost to herself. "Right, Dizzy?"

"Almost." I smile. "Then yours, the day after." She gasps, hiding her grin in my dark red dress. "Isn't that awesome?"

I readjust Holly so that she's resting on my right hip, my left leg already hurting from just walking to the church.

But the walk is worth it for how beautiful it is. The church still has its old gray stone walls and a floor that creaks with history. The stained-glass windows created centuries ago throw blocks of translucent rainbows across the original pews at the slightest bit of light. Bibles and hymnals are tucked comfortably behind each pew. Now strings of evergreen garland line the walls and festive wreaths hang between each window.

"Peace be with you!" Father Benedetti greets us once the hymn concludes.

"And with your spirit," we echo back. Holly mumbles a

version of the words against my arm as we sit down. Father Benedetti begins his sermon, his voice as deep and as rich as the music Noah creates with his cello.

Noah.

I probably shouldn't be thinking about my boyfriend in church, especially during midnight Mass, but as Father Benedetti dives into his sermon on the miracle of Jesus's birth, Noah stays planted firmly in my brain. I wonder if he's awake, remembering how my lips fit against his.

It helps with the perpetual cycle of kneeling and standing. Father Benedetti instructs us to turn our hymnals to "O Come, O Come, Emmanuel," and I sag slightly against the uncomfortable wooden pew as everyone else around me gets to their feet.

"You can sit, Daisy," Nonna tells me, laying her hand on my arm as she cuddles a passed-out Holly against her chest.

Then why do we stand at all?

I smile at her. "Thanks, Nonna."

I'm flipping through my hymnal for the page number printed in the program when a man's voice makes a chill race along my skin. "You know," he says haughtily, "she should stand with the rest of us. It's disrespectful to the Lord."

I straighten my spine. Each vertebra clicks into place as I look up. He's not anyone I recognize, but that's typical for midnight Mass. He's wearing an actual business suit, and his face is as red as his tie, trying to impress people who have no idea who he is.

"Excu—" Ma begins, biting down on the word. I'm surprised to see her jump to my defense, but since Holly is asleep, I guess she has the time.

"Sir, what's disrespectful is your ableism," I manage to fire back. "I'm pretty positive God doesn't care that I'm sitting."

The man puffs up like a bullfrog but turns to his own hymnal. We're both already a few bars behind the congregation. I find the hymn, boring my eyes into the onionskin pages as I ignore the feeling of my family's hands on my arms.

I'm not sure who touches me—Dad, Ma, Nonno, or Nonna, maybe all four of them—but I avoid their eyes, because I don't want to see their pity.

•   •   •

My mouth is still dry from the communion wafer, still sour from the wine, when we come back home. Without looking at any of the clocks we have in the apartment, I know it's almost two in the morning.

"Daisy," Dad whispers, cradling Holly, "I know it's late, sweetheart, but do you want to ta—"

"No." I sit down on the floor to unzip my boots and pull them off. "I'm just going to sleep out here, okay?"

My parents nod and continue down the hall to my and Holly's room, Ma saying that she'll at least bring out pajamas. I line my boots up with the rest of our shoes, walking into the living room and sitting down on the couch, taking a second to absorb the Christmas magic.

Our tree is in the corner, topped with a gold star, covered in white lights, red garland, and ornaments. Some of them are as old as both my parents, and some as young as me or Holly. I see the paper lamb I colored in during Sunday school when I was five. Ma punched a hole through the top and wound a string through so we could hang it on the tree. A miniature Christmas village is spread through the living room, silver garland framing its felt snow carpets. A train station; a church; a maple syrup shop; a Christmas tree farm; a glass pond with ice skaters frozen in motion. Pictures from past holiday seasons my parents display the day after Thanksgiving are on the walls: me as a tiny baby in a red Christmas dress; my parents and me posing in front of our Christmas tree, all of us beaming; and Holly in a sequined green dress on her first Christmas.

Ma brings out my slippers and a folded pair of pajamas—festive red ones with Scottish terriers that I got long before I had a boyfriend with a Scottish terrier, but that still make me miss Noah even more—along with my pink-and-yellow quilt.

"Even if you're sleeping out here, you should be comfortable," she murmurs, kissing the top of my head. "Remember, we have to be up early tomorrow, so get some sleep." We always see my uncle and cousin for breakfast on Christmas, but I think Ma just wanted to say something normal after what happened.

"Ti voglio bene, sweetheart."

"I love you, too, Ma." I hug her, and she kisses the top of my head again before shuffling down the hall to her and Dad's room. Changing into my pajamas, I leave my dress and tights draped over a kitchen chair. I know I could turn on the TV and look for a cheesy Christmas rom-com to lull me to sleep, but instead I wrap myself up in my quilt, grab my phone, and walk out onto our tiny terrace. Our wrought-iron patio furniture—a small table with a chipped blue mosaic pattern and love seat with matching cushions—are still damp from the last snowstorm, but I sit down anyway.

I click my phone to check the time: 2:15 a.m. Both Mazhar and Amal are sleeping. Even though they would put on their coats and hop on a train to get to me if I asked them to, I don't want to wake them up.

But Scotland is five hours ahead. Would Noah be awake now?

I call him on FaceTime. Noah picks up after a few rings, his dark hair tousled, adjusting his glasses. "Hi." He yawns. "What time is it back home?"

Home. My home is his home.

That's when I realize Noah isn't wearing a shirt.

He's hairier than I would've thought. Dark patches stand out against his pale chest. His arms are full of the same hair, too. I've never noticed before because he hides them underneath cardigans and sweaters and dress shirts.

"T-two," I say, a little flustered.

"Why are you still awa—" He doesn't finish that sentence before I cram my spastic left hand over my mouth, hot tears beginning to stream down my face. "Daisy." His voice is hard, but tender at the same time, anchoring me to my terrace, to the phone in my hand, to him, on the screen. "Tell me what's wrong. Please."

"It's *Christmas*," I blurt, realizing how absurd that sounds. Holly's going to wake us up soon. "Aren't you and your family celebrating?" Since he's been away, he's texted me pictures of elaborate breakfasts and, last night, a huge Christmas Eve dinner featuring a turkey.

"It's early. My brothers are probably still out on their morning run." He walks over to an oak dresser, pulling out a Royal Conservatoire of Scotland T-shirt and slipping it over his head. It's a little baggy, so it must not be his. "They let me sleep because of my medicine. I asked Dr. Singh about it yesterday. It's one of the side effects. We're opening presents after breakfast when they get back, and we're doing our annual trip down to Glasgow afterward. You don't need to worry about me. I'm fine right now. I'm worried about you, Daisy. You can talk to me. Whatever it is."

It's a short story when I tell him what happened at St. Vincent de Paul out loud, but this is just yet another chapter in how people view me because of my disability. And this was from a stranger, a jerk who's probably visiting his family in the best city in the world that he probably can't bring himself to enjoy.

And I'm *crying* over him. Over what he said. I've never cried about this in front of anyone but my family before.

It's a part of my life I feel more comfortable ignoring. It's so easy to distract myself when I am with my friends. They never view me as a disabled girl to be prayed for, or someone living with a seemingly impossible burden they wouldn't ever wish on anyone. To them, my cerebral palsy is as much a part of me as my violin.

But for some reason, with Noah, it's different. Maybe because he's been vulnerable with me, too.

Salt from my tears stings my eyes, my face feels prickly, and I'm gripping my quilt so tightly that my knuckles are turning white when I finish talking. Noah has been silent the entire time, and only when I'm wiping my face with my quilt does he speak. "I need to tell you something. Okay?"

I nod, sniffling.

"You are *not* what some pretentious asshole sees." Noah crosses the room, sitting down on a rumpled bed. "He doesn't know you and one day, you probably won't even remember him. He doesn't deserve to know you. Because you . . ." He pauses, his cheeks pink. "Daisy, you are *beautiful*. And knowing that—that *I* get to be with you again next week—just makes me so happy."

"Oh." I'm leaning against my phone, fresh tears rolling down my cheeks.

"Sorry." He's leaning against his phone, too, his voice a whisper. We'd be touching if it weren't for the Atlantic Ocean stretching between us. "Was that too much?"

"No." I close my eyes, smiling. Wishing he were on this terrace with me. "It was perfect."

"Then I'm glad." He sighs, and for the second time tonight, I remember what his lips felt like against mine. "Merry Christmas, Daisy."

"Merry Christmas, Noah."

CHAPTER NINETEEN
NOAH

On Christmas morning, we tear open the presents beneath a tree weighed down by gold and silver ornaments and eat enough food to supply the entire town of Portree. Later, my brothers pull me upstairs into the bedroom Douglas and I are sharing.

"What are you doing?" I ask as Douglas presses on the door to ensure that it's closed tightly.

Douglas glances at Gavin as he steps backward.

"We have another present for you," Gavin finishes, holding up a bag from Asda. "We didn't think to wrap it."

My eyebrows rise above my glasses, but I take the bag from him and look inside, then stare at both my brothers, as if they've sprouted three heads each. "Condoms," I say, as flatly as possible. "You bought me condoms for Christmas."

"It's a tradition," Douglas replies, sounding as though he and Gavin rehearsed this. Heat creeps up my back as he explains:

"I bought some for Gavin when he got his first girlfriend."

"But Daisy and I aren't—" I splutter.

"You never know when you'll need them," Gavin says. "It's smarter to have and not need them than to need and not have."

"You're bound for Juilliard," Douglas points out. "The whole family's known that since you were three. You don't want to potentially derail that."

"Look at you." Gavin chuckles, grinning at me. "You're so red! They're just condoms, Noah!"

"I know that!" I stash the grocery bag under my bed and straighten up before sitting on top of it.

"So." Gavin sits on the queen-size bed with Douglas, both of them looking at me with the same neutral expression. "How's therapy going?"

His question makes breakfast spoil in my stomach, and I hug my torso. "How do you know about that? Did Mom and Dad tell you?"

"You're our brother, of course they did. Was it supposed to be a secret?" Douglas spins his wedding band around on his ring finger. "Therapy is nothing to be ashamed of, you know."

Gavin nods, readjusting his slim, wire-framed glasses. "We just wanted to ask you how it's going," he continues calmly. "See if you wanted to talk about it. No judgment. Promise."

"Oh." I clear my throat. "Okay. Um." I drop my arms and rest them on my lap instead. "Thanks?"

"You're welcome." Gavin gives me a small smile. "I never

told you this." He blows out a breath between his teeth, and Douglas rubs his back. "I've been in therapy for years."

My mouth drops open, my glasses sliding down the bridge of my nose. "Really?"

"Yeah." Gavin nods. "Ever since I realized I wasn't"—he blinks up at the ceiling, almost like he doesn't want to cry—"ever since I realized that I was staying in Scotland, after I proposed to Isla."

"You've been in therapy for that long?" I ask. I feel the panic start to build in my chest. Gavin hasn't lived in America for years. *Will I be in therapy for that long, too?*

Gavin swallows. "Almost three years now. It's helped me so much that I decided to keep it up. So, you shouldn't feel embarrassed or alone, you know?" He smiles at me before the three of us get tangled in a group hug.

"Boys?" Dad knocks on the door, making all three of us jump. "Get your instruments. I want to take you somewhere."

•   •   •

I've never carried my cello through Glasgow's Christmas markets, a packed festival of endless lights, mouthwatering street food, and holiday cheer. With each step, my case repeatedly hits me in the shoulders. The Yorkshire pudding wrap filled with Christmas dinner trimmings is somehow not helping enough.

"Hey, Dad?" I ask once we pass the George Square Observation Wheel. "Why did you want us to bring our instruments?"

"You'll see." He beams, squeezing Mom's hand. Leading us away from the towering marble and granite City Chambers, down South Frederick Street and past McDonalds Bakers— the syrupy smell of baking fruit floating down the sidewalk—we soon arrive at a multistory building with curved windows, the name BRITANNIA stamped above the door.

"About time." Gavin grins at Dad. "I was wondering when you'd bring them here."

"An arcade?" Douglas peers into the pane of the doorway. "Why?"

"Not that." Dad shakes his head, stepping forward and leading us inside. "It's what's above it." He walks us through the dizzying candy-colored lights of the arcade and up a flight of creaky, narrow stairs that I'm positive we aren't supposed to have access to.

"Um." I bounce from one foot to the other as we reach the top of the stairs. The old wood groans beneath my boots. "Are we supposed to be here?"

" 'Course we are." Gavin readjusts his viola case on his shoulder. "The Britannia Panopticon's just a bit hidden from the rest of the world."

Dad steps through a heavy metal door, and we pile in after him, instrument cases jostling. The room has high ceilings and dusty brick walls with remnants of vaudeville posters pasted onto them. Its windows give way to the city down below.

"Irving!" Dad booms, nearly making me jump. "How are

you?" He's embracing a guy around his age with a potbelly and a neat red mustache.

"Lewis!" Irving beams at him. "So, you've decided to bring the rest of the family here, eh? Finally?"

"Well," Dad says heavily, "Noah's about to graduate in June, bound for Juilliard if he has anything to say about it, so I decided now would be perfect." My stomach flips at the mention of Juilliard, but I push it down.

"All right." Irving clears his throat. "It's so nice to finally meet you all. I'm your dad's oldest friend from university. Welcome to the Britannia Panopticon! This is the world's oldest surviving music hall. We still have events here, too," he adds. "Comedy nights, drag shows. But allow me to show you to a specific room. I can give you a tour afterward, sound good?"

Irving takes us through the music hall, our footsteps creaking eerily along with the rest of the building. I wonder what sort of performers came to this hall, if they were from music families like mine, if they carried expectations on their shoulders like I do.

We arrive in a room that's empty except for the stage. Murky sunlight streams in through windows across the wood. Posters are still pasted onto the walls, frozen here, like the performers don't want to leave.

"You want us to play here?" I look at my dad, my cello case weighing down on my spine.

Dad nods, his beard twitching with a smile. "Gavin has

already been here, of course." He gestures to his middle son, who smiles down at his feet. "But neither of you have. We've always been so busy when we visit. I *loved* it here when I was at the RCS, even just being around all this history. Go on, then." He nods toward the stage. "You haven't played your annual rendition of 'Carol of the Bells' yet."

Mom beams and takes our coats. Douglas and Gavin climb onstage, but I stay where I am. Before I know what's happening, I crumple to the old wood floor, my face in my hands. My cello case knocks me sharply on the back of the head, hard enough that lights pop in front of my eyes.

Light. I can barely see the sun streaming in through the windows anymore. It's just fuzzy against my vision, shrinking, like the amount of air my lungs can hold. Almost as if my heart is trying to push them out of my ribs.

"Noah!" A high voice cracks through my fog, and I blink back to reality. Mom is crouched on the floor in front of me. Her glasses are perched on the edge of her nose, her hair tumbling down around her face in the same curls she gave me. Her hands are on my face. I can feel the coldness of her wedding band on my cheek, and that simple thing is what grounds me. "Love? Are you okay?"

"Yeah." I rub my eyes under my glasses, blinking again. Above her head, I can see Dad right behind her. Douglas, Gavin, and Irving are grouped together at the base of the stage, all of them with identical worry in their eyes. Gavin asks if I need to go to the hospital. "I—I'm okay. Anxiety attack."

"Was it something I said?" Dad asks, concerned.

"No," I say quickly, trying to reassure him. "It wasn't just one thing. It's just. I'm not sure."

"Be sure to mention this to Dr. Singh at your next appointment, okay?" he responds, helping me to my feet. "Between this and how tired you have been, maybe you need to change your medication?"

"Are you up for playing?" Mom asks, her brow knitted.

"Yeah." I nod. "I want to."

My brothers and I climb onstage, unpack our instruments, and run rosin along our bows.

"So!" Gavin's voice suddenly bounces off the bricks, joining the dozens of performers who were here before us. "Now that we have you up here, tell us about Daisy."

I nearly drop my rosin stick.

"You didn't say anything when we rehearsed last night," Douglas points out.

"Excuse me?" I distract myself by tuning my strings. "Do you want me to play or talk about my girlfriend?"

"Both?" Douglas suggests. "You've been avoiding—"

"No," I say, proving his point. "Let's play."

We launch into "Carol of the Bells," each of our separate instruments filling the room the way they can't a traditional auditorium. Douglas's violin, Gavin's viola, and my cello reverberate against bricks filled with the sound of music played here before ours, flowing back to us.

Growing up, I thought music was the only thing I needed. I didn't need friends, or a girlfriend. I didn't need a life out from behind my cello. I was an island, a Manhattan of my own making.

Until November. Until Daisy. Until Mazhar. Until Amal. Maybe I had been wrong all along.

Performing with Daisy was the best I've ever felt. Maybe it's not *just* about the music.

As we play the final notes, words leave my lips, the way music just left my strings: "I want to perform with her again."

"That's how you feel about her?" Gavin asks as everyone claps.

"Yeah." I look away from my brothers' shiny eyes, instead at the strands of horsehair dangling from my bow as if they won't notice the color in my cheeks that way. "It's simple. But that's how I feel." I smile. "Does that make sense?"

"Love makes the most sense when it is simple," Gavin points out. "It doesn't have to be 'Carol of the Bells' from memory, Noah."

Love. Am I in love with her already? I lean into my cello, the scroll digging into my shoulder as I realize: I've been falling in love with Daisy this entire time.

CHAPTER TWENTY
DAISY

The rest of winter break passes in a blur of party poppers and junk food. I missed Noah most while watching the ball drop on New Year's Eve in Amal's apartment.

On our first day back at school I am so focused on his arrival later tonight that I don't hear what Mrs. Sharma assigned for homework.

"We have to read the next chapter of *The Age of Exploration* and answer the six questions at the end." Mazhar laughs. "Do you have Noah on the brain?"

I smirk as we reach my locker. "Like you don't think about Amal all the time?"

I gather the other books I need for tonight's homework, cram my knit wool hat over my hair, and button up my coat.

"I do think about her all the time," Mazhar admits, "but I have not missed a homework assignment over it. At least not this year."

"This is the first school day of the new year," I say.

"My point still stands, Daisy!" Mazhar grins, walking us down the hall. "Come on. Amal is meeting us at the Madison Square Park Shake Shack."

Immediately thoughts of Noah share brain space with a cheeseburger and chocolate custard shake, despite it being below freezing outside. At least it's sunny today, so sitting in the park should be nice.

We're almost to the front doors when Mazhar stops. "I forgot my AP Music Theory textbook."

"Subconsciously?" I ask. *The Harmonies of Advanced Music Theory* is over eight hundred pages and hardcover. It's kind of hard to forget. I'm surprised my copy hasn't severed my spine.

"Perhaps." Mazhar shrugs. "Wait for me outside, I'll be right there." He smiles at me and pivots on his heel while I hike up my backpack and push through the glass door.

"Hi, Daisy." I blink against the winter sunlight and see that Noah is standing on the sidewalk, his hands in the pockets of his peacoat.

"You're back already?" A blush that I'm positive has absolutely nothing to do with the cold spills across my cheeks. "I thought your flight landed tonight. Why didn't you text me?"

"And ruin the surprise?"

We run toward each other. Noah easily scoops me up into his arms and spins us around.

"I've missed you," I murmur, pressing my forehead against his.

"I've missed you, too." He smiles before kissing me, his lips sweet and warm.

"Daisy, Noah!" Imani, a senior musical theater student, runs up to us, her braids bouncing on her backpack. "I didn't get to tell you: Your performance at the concert was amazing! My little sister wants to play the cello now."

"That's awesome." Noah smiles at her, his cheeks pink.

"Thanks, Imani." I grin back at her, and she waves goodbye.

"Great!" Mazhar sings, joining us again. "You found each other."

"Wait." I take Noah's hand in mine, leaning into his coat, needing to be as close as possible after being an ocean apart. "*You knew!* And you said nothing!"

"*The Harmonies of Advanced Music Theory* was in my backpack this whole time." Mazhar winks at me, looking over at Noah. "Amal is excited to see you," he adds as we head toward the subway station.

"I can't believe you, Mazhar!" I laugh, Noah squeezing my hand. "I would tell *you* if Amal came back early. It's what best friends do."

"Best friends also allow each other to have romantic moments with their significant other," Mazhar points out. "I was doing you a *solid* . . ."

His voice trails off as his gaze latches onto one of the many screens crowding Times Square. Advertisements for Broadway productions outside their theaters, a screen over the M&M's store featuring a giant green M&M watching the humans below.

But Mazhar is looking at a screen featuring me and Noah performing our duet at the winter holiday concert.

"Why are you guys up there?" he asks in a slow voice.

"Oh my God—" Noah croaks, tense beside me, his knuckles like rocks in my palm.

I can't say anything, so I just grab my phone from my coat pocket. Trying to push past the muscle spasms snaking down my legs, I navigate to the YouTube app, ready to search for the Manhattan Academy of Musical Performance's channel.

But instead, I see a thumbnail of me and Noah frozen in motion as we perform our duet onstage. I tap on it, my mind blank. Our school's YouTube channel is never on the front page.

I take my finger off the phone screen and see why we are now: Our duet has 400,000 views.

"Daisy." Noah's voice is hoarse, but also the loudest sound I've ever heard.

Murmurs crescendo around us from the perpetually busy street. Conversations turn toward us. Me and Noah.

"Canım." I didn't even realize Mazhar was calling Amal, but of course he would. "Change of plans. Can you meet us at Café Istanbul?"

Mazhar leads us through Times Square, not stopping until we reach his parents' restaurant. I'm reeling too much to care about how my legs feel like they're on fire from how fast we've walked.

"Anne, Baba!" Mazhar yells, the bell tinkling above his head as the door slams behind us. "We've got a problem. Daisy and Noah's duet went viral!"

Luckily, it's before the dinner rush, so Café Istanbul is almost empty.

"What happened?" Kemal asks, his mustache twitching as he and Sabah bustle out of the kitchen.

"Is anyone hurt?" Sabah follows up, dusting her hands off on her apron. Her eyes rove over each of us, and satisfied, she asks if anyone is hungry.

I was. But now there's a brick sitting in my stomach.

Mazhar says something to them in Turkish, pulling his phone out from his coat pocket and showing his parents. "They were recognized," he adds in English for our benefit.

"What are we going to do?" Noah asks, and I realize this is the first time he's spoken since we saw ourselves on-screen.

"Just take a moment to breathe," Mazhar explains. "This place is awesome but tiny. No one's going to find you. Not with Ripley's and Madame Tussauds around. Sometimes tourist bait comes in handy."

Sabah nods, surveying us with kind eyes. "Daisy, Noah, you can hide out in the kitchen, just in case someone comes by. Mazhar, you may as well help out."

"Amal is coming," Mazhar explains. For a moment, Noah

and I just stand there, listening to the hustle and bustle outside the kitchen.

Amal arrives at the restaurant soon after, rushing past her boyfriend for the first time in my memory, and over to the service window.

"Mazhar texted me everything!" She holds up her phone, beaming. "You went viral! It's so exciting!"

"Exciting?" I repeat, incredulous. "Amal, it's the opposite of exciting."

"Wait. Why?" Amal presses, practically bouncing up and down. "I think it's amazing! You're kind of like celebrities!"

"Well, we don't want to be!" I burst out, my voice thick with tears. But my stomach twists when I see the hurt in Amal's eyes. "I'm sorry—"

"I'll be right out here," Amal interjects. She goes to sit down with Sabah, discussing shades of yellow for the menus. Mazhar tells his dad about surprising me with Noah. Their laughter makes me smile for a second.

Noah wraps me up in his arms as I sit down on a stool. His voice has come back to him now, more confident. He smells like cinnamon. Warm and lovely. "What are we supposed to do?"

I shake my head against him as I loop my arms around his waist. "How did we go viral?" I murmur.

Noah smiles against my forehead before he kisses it. "The internet is . . . weird?" he suggests.

"True." I laugh just a little as I settle my ear against his chest, listening to his heartbeat.

"A couple hundred views is normal for the academy," he adds.

"Yeah, but not—"

"Coming up: Take a look at the viral video that's been sweeping the internet," a cheery voice says from the front of the restaurant. Noah and I rush to the service window. He lifts me up onto the toes of his boots so that I can see over. Our gazes fix on the TV mounted to the wall, tuned to a commercial for *The Hope Baker Hour.*

The fact that Times Square Broadcast Studios, where it's filmed, is just down the block makes this worse.

Kemal goes to turn off the Turkish music. Mazhar's fingers are frozen on his apron strings. Sabah and Amal have left papers on the table in front of them.

A slim woman beams on-screen. Her honey-blond hair is tied back into a bun. She's wearing a pink gingham button-down, light blue jeans, and pristine white sneakers. Her set, all silver leather furniture, with matching columns framing a picture of the New York City skyline, fades away to our duet, the volume muted so that she can continue her commentary. "Daisy and Noah, seniors at the Manhattan Academy of Musical Performance, have wowed the world with their performance," she continues.

"Both are reportedly hoping to attend Juilliard, and of

course, it's easy to see why. But what is perhaps the most interesting is the fact that, according to the comments section, Daisy Abano is the only violinist with cerebral palsy to have attended the school. She is undeniably an inspiration to musicians everywhere, and to the rest of the world." Applause and cheers burst from the audience.

That word. Again.

I fall back, thinking I'm about to crash onto the floor, but instead hit Noah's chest. He catches me around the waist, his hands clasping together.

"This is why it's the opposite of exciting," I whisper. "This isn't happening."

"I know." Noah's voice is the G string on my violin: low, dependable, the foundation for so many songs.

It's the only thing holding me together right now, knowing that he's right here.

I edge over the partition again, and Noah and I watch Kemal changing the channels to different stations. Same footage. Almost the same words, as if everyone is reading from a singular script. *Inspiring. Overcoming. Despite her disability* . . .

My muscles get tighter with every useless, empty spin on my existence.

The only comfort is that the school edited our performance down to the duet, choosing not to include the epic kiss we shared afterward. At least that isn't being shared across every TV station in the city.

"Daisy." Noah's whisper sends a shiver down my neck. "Do you want to stay with me tonight?"

Stay with him. As in, be in the same apartment, potentially sleeping in the same bed. A hundred thoughts about what that all means fly through my mind. But I just don't want to be without him tonight.

"Yes."

A shrill ringing from my backpack echoes off the tile walls. I step off Noah's boots, grabbing my phone from the front pouch of my backpack. It's my mom. Ottavia's Flower Arrangements doesn't have a TV, but Ma browses Facebook, sending me dog videos in between orders.

We could be on there, too. We probably are.

"Daisy?" she asks when I accept the call. "Sweetheart, have you seen the TV? Mrs. Valentini"—at least it's not Mrs. Pecora, not yet—"she texted your nonna, who texted me. She said you're on *The Hope Baker Hour* because of your concert. This is wonderful! Think about the opportunities—"

"Ma." I walk back over to the partition, Noah helping me lean out into the restaurant again. There's another news report on the duet, this one from Scotland. The BBC logo burns into my eyes. "I saw. I'm in Café Istanbul right now. Can I stay in Manhattan, please? I don't want to go all the way back to Brooklyn tonight."

She's silent. I'm expecting her to say that she can just pick me up on the way home from the shop, so before she can, I add: "Amal invited me." *As if she wants to talk to me right now.*

I keep my eyes on Noah, who takes my hand in his. Even though Mazhar and I have spent countless nights sprawled out in Amal's living room, marathoning anime and eating cheese curls until all our fingers turn orange, I don't have any intention of even asking her.

Lying to my mom is easier since I've suddenly become an inspiration to the entire world.

CHAPTER TWENTY-ONE
NOAH

"I'm home!" I announce, even though I don't have to. I could hear their whispers change to frenzied conversation when we walked into the apartment. "Daisy's with me."

On cue, my parents abandon the living room to meet us in the hallway. Mom darts underneath Dad's arm to be in front. "Have you seen?" She doesn't finish the sentence; she doesn't need to.

"Yeah." Daisy squeezes my hand when I answer. I give her one in return as I explain how we were recognized even before we knew our duet had spread like an unquenchable wildfire.

"Here." Dad turns around, leading us into the kitchen. He starts getting tea ready for us. "Two spoonfuls of sugar and a bit of milk, right, my love?" he asks Daisy kindly.

"Please." Daisy smiles, and I do, too, just a little. He remembers how she takes her tea.

We all settle with our red mugs at the dining table just outside the kitchen, a plate of chocolate chip sea salt caramel shortbread cookies between us. Mom leans over the glass piece, her hands cradling her mug, biting her lip. Her eyes stray to a spot away from us. Judging by the jingling noise, Haggis has come to inspect what's going on.

"Mackenzie," Dad murmurs, tossing Haggis a dog biscuit from the treat jar we have as a centerpiece. "Maybe we should wait, my love."

"It's best they go in knowing already." Mom sighs, creating ripples across her tea.

"Know what?" Daisy asks shakily. "What else is there?"

Mom's quiet for a moment as we all listen to Haggis crunching on his snack. "The academy called us. Your principal, Mr. Loman, specifically." She turns her eyes to Daisy. "I'm sure he's calling your parents, too. He wants to meet with all of us and Ms. Silverstein tomorrow afternoon at one o'clock. I just wanted to let you both know so it doesn't come as a surprise."

Mom takes a cookie from the plate but spins it around in her fingers instead of biting into it. "Would you like some privacy to call your parents, Daisy? Lewis and I can—"

"No." Daisy sputters into her tea, pounding on her chest for a second. "They'll call me if they need to. They're probably still at work."

Dad wipes cookie crumbs from his beard with a napkin. "Your parents don't know you're here, do they, my love?" he asks finally.

"No," Daisy mumbles, her cheeks turning pink for an entirely different reason.

"We haven't seen each other since before Scotland," I chime in. "It was my idea. I invited her to stay over."

My parents stare, unblinking. I don't think either of them was prepared for this.

"Well, Daisy, of course you're welcome to stay here," Mom replies. "I don't feel comfortable lying to your parents. But I suppose this is a strange situation. We won't make a habit of it. And, Noah, you'll sleep on the couch and give Daisy your bed. Lend her some pajamas, too."

"I'll make everyone breakfast tomorrow," Dad adds. "I have a feeling we'll need it."

• • •

Later that night, as I'm lying on the couch, curled up beneath a thick quilt Grandma Fiona knitted, Haggis at my feet, a text wakes me up from the sleep I'm finally slipping into. I'm not sure what time it is, but Manhattan still rumbles on the streets below, unable to sleep itself.

Daisy (2:45 a.m.): Can you come in here, please? I can't sleep.

I get up from the couch and walk out of the living room, upstairs to my bedroom, the quilt flowing around me like a cape. Haggis is trotting behind. I'm grateful my parents are heavy sleepers; otherwise his tags would wake them up. My heart thrums against my sternum when I see Daisy sitting up in my bed, surrounded by silver light, half swallowed up by the pajamas I lent her.

"Hi," I whisper. *She's in my apartment, in my bedroom, in the middle of the night. She's so beautiful.*

She raises her hand, waving. "Hi."

I carefully shut the door before crossing the room and sitting on my bed. Daisy cuddles into me, and I fold the quilt around us. "How are we supposed to play after this?" Tears well up at the bottoms of her eyes, and I use the edge of the quilt to wipe them away.

"By playing anyway," I tell her. "You are an *incredible* violinist. You know that, right?"

"Yeah." Daisy's voice is lost, almost like a rest in a piece. "I actually do."

We're both quiet for a moment. I hold Daisy close, tucking her beneath my chin as we listen to each other's breathing. The last time we did this, we were in our separate apartments.

But here, I can *feel* her breathing. Her body against mine, her hands in mine, her heartbeat from her fingertips.

"We should get some sleep," she says, her voice muffled against my pajama shirt.

CHAPTER TWENTY-TWO
DAISY

Noah starts to get up to leave, but I hold him in place. "Stay," I whisper. "If that's okay."

"It's fine." Noah kisses my forehead and settles back against the pillows.

I snake my hands up into his hair, and he presses his lips to mine. My breath hitches in my throat.

If we were in the orchestra's storage room, Noah would stop here.

Except we're in the darkness of his bedroom, and our lips aren't leaving each other's.

I was alone in this bed just a few minutes ago, praying that I'd fall asleep, that dreams would carry me away from what we saw in Times Square. But when Noah moves on top of me, the weight of his body pressing mine into his blue bedspread, I've never been more awake.

Noah kicks the quilt to the floor as his mouth travels down my neck. I move backward, leaning into his pillows, pulling him closer with each press of his lips. The fingers on my left hand tangle in his hair. My right hand moves the T-shirt aside, letting his kisses cover my bare shoulder.

His fingers drift from the waistband of the pajama pants I borrowed from him, slipping beneath the T-shirt and skimming up along my sides. His touch sends a fire spreading through the rest of my body, making my left side seize up in a muscle spasm I actually don't despise.

"Noah." I sigh.

"Daisy?" His voice is scratchy and exhausted around his sharp breath as he gazes down at me. His lips are swollen from our kisses. His hair is tousled from my hands, falling into his eyes, which are the color of forget-me-nots even with only the silver light of the Upper East Side cascading through his window to illuminate his face.

"Yeah?" I whisper.

"Do you want to . . . " Noah's voice trails off, and we re-adjust ourselves in his bed, me in his lap, his fingertips resting on my hips.

I lean my forehead against his, feeling his breath on my lips. We've had the most surreal few hours. It won't be long before all of New York knows our names, something neither of us is pre-pared for.

And we aren't prepared to have sex, either.

"No."

Noah's eyes crinkle at their corners. His fingers slide out from underneath my T-shirt, holding the hem now instead.

"This is so new to me," I continue. "*We* are so new. I'm not ready yet. I've always been taught that sex is something . . ." I pause while I try to find the right words and kiss his forehead since I can actually reach it for a change. "I don't think I see it happening in the near future."

"That's okay." He kisses my forehead in return. "If we ever have sex, it will be because it's something both of us want. Do you want me to go back to the living room?"

"Can you stay here?" I wrap my arms around his shoulders. "Please?"

"Absolutely." Noah falls backward until we're lying on his bed. I move closer until my ear is against his chest. "What are you doing?" he murmurs.

"Listening to your heartbeat," I reply softly, hearing the strong, steady thrum. "I love the sound. It calms me down."

Noah falls quiet. I pull away from him a little to meet his eyes. His brows are knitted, like they were when I first explained cerebral palsy to him. Only this time I can practically see the words tumbling around inside his head.

"Is that weird?" I ask.

"I don't think so," Noah whispers finally. "I'm *glad*, actually. I never thought I could do that for someone."

He presses a kiss to the crown of my head before we drift off to sleep.

And hours later, we wake up to the sunrise peeking through his curtains, our limbs tangled together, my ear pressed to his chest again.

CHAPTER TWENTY-THREE
NOAH

When we wake up, my parents are in the kitchen making tea, waffles, and bacon. So, they definitely know that we secretly slept in the same bed. No one so much as glances at the empty couch when we walk in and sit at the table. I know I'm going to hear about this later.

On our way to school, my anxiety rattles around in my brain with every step.

"Do you think we're in trouble?" Daisy sits down in the small seating area reserved for seniors and disabled people, while I stand in front of her, holding the pole.

"We could be?" I settle on saying. The train rockets out of Grand Central, and I only lurch slightly. People in business suits and expensive blouses rub their eyes before returning to their phones or mass-market paperbacks.

If anyone on here recognizes us, they're probably too tired to say anything. Or they could just be the sort of battle-hardened New Yorkers who are so used to the concept of absurd celebrity that they don't care. I mean, once you've witnessed a guy in nothing but his underwear and a cowboy hat playing the guitar during a snowstorm in Times Square, I guess you've seen everything.

Daisy reaches for my hand, clutching her violin to her chest. I bring her fingers to my lips, kissing them. "Even if we are in trouble," she continues, "the bright side is, we're too viral for Principal Loman to expel us, I guess? *The Hope Baker Hour* would have a field day."

• • •

As much as I want to hold Daisy's hand before we walk into Principal Loman's office after lunch, I don't. Neither of us even pushes the door open to the main office; we just stand out in the hallway, looking through its glass windows.

At the Manhattan Academy of Musical Performance, you quickly become accustomed to the constant sounds: songs, tuning, the press of piano keys, laughter, footsteps, lessons on molecular biology, violin practices, and so on. But the sound of clearing my own throat is so sharp that I jump, shivers cascading down my back. "Sorry." I stare down at my sneakers. "What do you think he'll bring up first? The kiss or the fact that BuzzFeed is calling us an internet sensation?"

"We're on *BuzzFeed* now?" Daisy says, staring at me.

"Yeah, Mazhar showed it to me," I explain. "He's been

keeping track on the internet to see what people are saying about us."

Daisy blows out a breath from between her teeth and closes her eyes.

"How long before we are a hashtag? This is a nightmare."

I reach out and thread my fingers through hers. Together, we push through the main office doors, and are waved into Principal Loman's office by a secretary.

The walls of Principal Loman's office are covered in school awards. His master's degrees in musical performance (from Juilliard, because of course) and education (from Columbia because, again, of course) are displayed proudly behind his massive oak desk. The only personal, non-accomplishments-related touch is a picture of his wife, a principal flutist from Toronto, and son posing together at a March of Dimes walk, his son grinning from the seat of his lime-green wheelchair.

"Daisy!" Principal Loman stands up from his leather chair, greeting us as if we're alumni paying him a visit. "Noah! How wonderful to see you. Please, take a seat."

"Hi, love." Mom's hand lands on my shoulder and I almost jump again. I was so worried that I forgot our parents were going to be here. But they're standing off to the side of the room, offering us smiles. Ms. Silverstein, seated behind them, is uncharacteristically stiff.

"Hi, Mom." Daisy and I sit down in the plush leather seats, letting go of each other's hands immediately.

"So." Principal Loman folds his hands before leaning across his desk. "You two put on quite the performance at the winter concert. Your duet aside."

"What do you *mean* our duet aside?" I suddenly blurt out. *How can he just say that so casually?* "The duet *was* the performance, and that performance was important. We're both waiting on callbacks for Juilliard auditions. Faculty was in the audience." I'm quiet for a second before adding: "Sir."

"Noah." Principal Loman looks at me, raising a pale blond eyebrow, his blue eyes shimmering. "Please don't misconstrue why I called this meeting. It's obvious to everyone in this room, and those who were in the auditorium that night, that you possess great talent. Both of you. And." He grins. "I have no doubt Juilliard will be contacting you about live auditions. But I must ask: Have you seen the attention that video has received?"

We're everywhere, I want to say. *The news, YouTube, Twitter, Instagram, BuzzFeed, The Hope Baker Hour.* But I stay quiet instead.

"Of course they have," Ms. Silverstein says in a surprisingly snappy tone. "They're teenagers. The internet's in their hands wherever they go."

"Right, of course." Principal Loman holds up his hand, swiveling his iMac around so that we can see the dozen different tabs he has open. I lean forward to read them better. "The attention seems to go further than just you two." He looks over at Daisy, as if he's seeing her for the first time, his eyes zeroing in on her left hand bunched around the hem of her skirt. She fidgets, her leg jiggling against mine, and I wonder if she's even more nervous about being here than I am.

"People all over the internet are being drawn to the academy," he continues. "They want to know more about the work that we do here, where Noah and Daisy are becoming the cellist and violinist they were destined to be. Of course"—he chuckles—"I must add that kissing onstage is frowned upon unless a performance dictates it."

I'm pink from my hairline down to my toes. I glance at Daisy. She is, too.

"But that aside." Principal Loman waves his hand. *Teenagers and their hormones*, he's probably thinking. "This is all fantastic publicity for the school, so I really must thank you. Parents, you should be proud of your children. Ms. Silverstein, you should be proud of your students."

"Can we leave please, sir?" Daisy's voice is small. "I need to get to Music History."

"I have Ear Training," I add, my eyes focused on the diploma from Juilliard hanging above our principal's head.

"Very well." Principal Loman claps his hands. "But before you go." He touches a tab on his monitor. It opens to *The Hope Baker Hour*'s homepage, a mess of pastel blues, pinks, and glitter tossed over the New York City skyline. Hope Baker herself is beaming as brightly as the top of the Empire State Building touched by sunlight. Principal Loman sits back in his chair, his spine perfect against the leather, his grin back in place. "We have received requests for a TV appearance. *The Hope Baker Hour* wants to do a featurette on Noah and Daisy. Her team proposed January fourteenth. I'd of course excuse you both from school for the day."

My mouth drops open. This is amazing. *Imagine what appearing on a show like this could do for my career. For both of us.* But my stomach twists when Daisy's fingers weave themselves through mine again. She hates all this attention.

"That's the same week we find out about our Juilliard auditions," she says softly. Suddenly I feel a little dizzy. I grip Daisy's hand harder, and she squeezes mine back.

"So, they want us to go on the show," Daisy says, her voice steady now.

"Well, of course." Principal Loman's eyes meet hers. *Am I imagining things, or is he speaking to her more slowly?* "But we'll need your parents' permission." He clears his throat, looking at our parents and our orchestra conductor. "Now, what do you all think of this opportunity?"

• • •

Principal Loman's words pound against my skull for the rest of the day, even when Daisy, Mazhar, Amal, and I are all sprawled out around Mazhar's living room later that afternoon.

"Your principal is an asshole," Amal says simply, taking a sip of her soda.

"He is." Daisy pauses the episode of anime that had just

started playing on-screen. "But I thought you liked the idea of all this happening. Didn't you want your best friend to be wildly famous and on television?"

"We're back to this again?" Amal arches her eyebrow. "I get all the reasons you hate this. But I also see the ways it could be good for you! Sorry if I'm *excited* for my friends." Her brown skin flushes as Mazhar wraps his arms around her shoulders.

"Maybe it's because I was in Times Square with them," Mazhar chimes in. "And I saw how Daisy and Noah"—he gestures to me with his can of lemonade—"reacted to seeing themselves on-screen, but if I hadn't been there, I might have had the same thoughts as you, Amal."

"You would've been excited for us?" I take a sip from my own lemonade.

"Well, yeah." Mazhar shrugs. "It's not every day *orchestra* musicians explode, you know? Much less your friends. I can see where Amal's coming from."

Daisy nods. She's put her soda on a coaster and is now playing with her hands in her lap. But her gaze is fixed on Amal. "I know. I get it," she murmurs. "I'm sorry."

"I'm sorry, too." Amal gets up from the sectional and walks over to Daisy, the two of them hugging each other tightly.

"You know what this party needs? Snacks," Daisy says when she and Amal let go. "I can go get some."

"You know where everything is," Mazhar replies, grinning as Amal snuggles next to him. "Grab something good."

Daisy walks into the kitchen, and I follow her, watching as she heads right for the pantry. "What's up?" she asks, her arms filled with bags of chips, jars of onion dip and salsa, and two kinds of Oreos.

"I thought you might want some help." I laugh, taking the Oreos from her.

"Now I do," she chuckles. "This is one of the only times, though. Thanks."

"Noted." I nod, clearing my throat. "Uh, Daisy?"

"Yeah?" She raises an eyebrow at me, smiling just a little.

"Would you like to go out on a date with me to Carnegie Hall?" I ask. Her mouth falls open. "Friday at seven? Douglas is performing."

"I would love to," she murmurs, breathless. "But do you really think that's a good idea? We've just gone *viral*. We don't want to draw attention to ourselves."

"Of course we don't," I agree. "But what better place to hide than in plain sight?"

CHAPTER TWENTY-FOUR
DAISY

There isn't an official dress code, but it's *Carnegie Hall*! We aren't just going to wear the same outfits we wear to school. Noah's swapped out his khakis and layered sweater for a pair of black slacks and an aquamarine dress shirt. I've changed out of my jeans and sweater into a black skirt, opaque tights, and an aquamarine blouse Amal let me borrow.

She insisted we be color coordinated.

We're not flashy enough to draw attention, but enough that tonight feels special.

Noah weaves his fingers through mine as we gaze up at the building's tiers of arched windows that seem to glare down at us and invite us in at the same time. The whole building is illuminated yellow in the night, a beacon of music right here on Seventh Avenue.

"Wow." My breath flows from my mouth in a fog. "It's incredible."

"Yeah." Noah squeezes my hand. "It is. Ready to go inside?"

"Wait, hang on." I blow out another breath, giddiness making goose bumps sprout up along my arms. "Let's take a selfie. Here." I pull my phone out from a silver clutch and hand it to him. "You do it. Your arms are longer than mine."

"Sure thing." Noah grins, taking it from me and holding it up in front of us. "Ready?"

I move closer to him, and he winds his free arm around my waist. "Ready."

"Okay." Before he snaps the picture, Noah swoops in and kisses my cheek, making me laugh. That moment is now frozen on my phone: us in front of Carnegie Hall, yellow light all around, a laugh in my mouth, and a smile on my boyfriend's lips.

I make someone this happy. I make Noah *this happy.*

I post the photo to Instagram and immediately get likes from Mazhar and Amal. "Shall we go in now?" Noah asks, still beaming.

"Absolutely."

Noah leads us through the doors and into the Stern Auditorium, the grandest performance hall in the place. Tiers of plush red velvet seats encased by white walls rise to the ceiling, overseen by a gleaming chandelier. The opulence makes my heart soar and my stomach drop simultaneously. I know that I belong in a place like this, but I also never thought that I would get the chance to step inside.

It's the most beautiful theater I've ever seen. The kind of place

I perform in when I'm dreaming. Stage lights on me, wearing a black dress that cascades to the floor like a waterfall as I fill the room with my violin. High, piercing Es; deep, almost mournful Gs; and every note in between. Everyone applauds me as I bow. Not because I am "inspiring," but because I am talented.

Except I'm not dreaming. I'm actually *here*, with my boyfriend.

After we sit in our seats in the center mezzanine, I turn to Noah, our hands clasped together on the armrest between us. My eyes flit back and forth between the majestic view and the lights dancing across my boyfriend's lenses.

"Can I ask you something?" we say in unison.

"You go first," I say.

Noah readjusts his glasses, then lets go of my hand to put his arm around me instead. "How do you actually feel about going on *The Hope Baker Hour*?"

"Honestly?" Leaning into the smooth silk of his shirt, I listen to the low rumble of his breath, the beat of his heart beneath my ear. "I don't know. I *know* it would be a great opportunity for us, so there's that, at least. But I'm really unsure about the rest. I mean, she doesn't want me on to play. She wants me on because I'm disabled." I leave out the part of the meeting that made me more uncomfortable than anything else: how Principal Loman, the man responsible for me attending the Manhattan Academy of Musical Performance in the first place, still feels the need to treat me differently from Noah. "Can I ask my question now?"

"Go ahead."

I wrap my right arm around his front, cuddling as much as we can while we're in separate chairs. "Is it weird for you to be back after you performed here?"

A beat of silence passes between us. "It's always a little weird," Noah admits. "Everything about being at one of the most famous music venues in the world is weird. I was prepared as I could be, but . . ."

"You were only eleven," I finish for him after a beat of silence.

"Exactly," he says. "You'll be as prepared, as rehearsed as you can get, right? And there are those moments where everything will go perfectly."

I lift up my head to smile at him. "Like our duet."

"Like our duet," he repeats, nuzzling his forehead against mine. "But there are also times where the nerves just get to you, you know? Granted, I was still a kid. I didn't know what to make of anything beyond my cello."

"And are you starting to now?" I ask, closing my eyes when he presses his lips to mine. Just once. Enough for a date where we're blending in with the rest of the theater.

"With a little help from therapy and medicine?" Noah runs his fingers along my shoulder, and I curl into him. "Yeah."

"Good." I kiss his jaw, my eyes crinkling when he smiles. "I'm glad."

The lights dim. The audience applauds as Douglas takes the

stage, dressed all in black. He looks exactly like Noah, except for the gorgeous violin in his hand. After bowing to the audience, Douglas positions his violin beneath his chin, raises his bow, and begins to play. Watching him onstage, bathed in golden light, is something else. He belongs there; he captivates the audience with every note he plays. His shivering vibrato, his perfect bow movements, the way he closes his eyes at points because he knows the song that well, is extraordinary. Someone with that much talent, showing me the height of performance I'll some-day reach, displayed down on that stage.

It's no wonder Noah puts so much pressure on himself.

The house lights come back on an hour later, and I blink against their brightness.

Noah grips my hand tightly in his as we walk down the mezzanine's stairs. He leads us not toward a bustling Manhattan night, but down the hall and deeper into the venue.

"Where are we going?" I ask, our shoes echoing as we walk across the shiny tiled floor.

"To say hi."

Noah knocks on a door, stepping back as Douglas pulls it open, immediately embracing his brother. "Did you enjoy the show?" he asks, polishing his glasses with the hem of his black dress shirt.

"Enjoy it?" I repeat. "Douglas, you're *incredible*! I've never heard the violin played like that before."

"Well, that's very kind." He slips his glasses back on his face, smiling at me. "Thank you." His blue eyes gleam. "Is my brother treating you well?"

I laugh at the same time Noah sputters.

"Yes," I say finally.

"As he should." Douglas ruffles Noah's hair.

Noah steps away from his brother, but he's smiling. "Do you think the auditorium's empty now?"

"I believe so." Douglas buttons up his wool coat, slinging his violin case over his shoulder. Noah squeezes my hand. "Follow me."

Douglas leads us from his dressing room to the cool, darkened backstage area of the Stern Auditorium. After peeking out into the house, he looks at us over his shoulder. "It's empty," he says. "Go on ahead."

"What?" I stare from my boyfriend to his brother. "We—we can go *onstage*?"

"I was hoping we would be able to." Noah raises our intertwined hands, kissing my knuckles, and I smile up at him. "Wait. Close your eyes."

Shutting my eyes, I let Noah lead me out onto the stage, where his brother was performing just minutes before. Our footsteps echo up to the auditorium's glorious chandelier, playing a music all their own.

"Okay," Noah says. "Open your eyes, Daisy."

Sitting in the audience, viewing its splendor from your seat, is an experience I never thought I'd have. The view of the theater rising up to the ceiling from center stage is one I never thought I'd see. I never imagined my dreams filled with beautiful black dresses, music from my violin, and pulsing lights at my back would be anything more than a fantasy. Not when I remembered how much that particular future costs.

Sure, I'm talented enough to exist alongside Noah in our world of orchestral music, but I'm not as privileged as he is. If I weren't dating him, I wouldn't be standing here right now. I'm so grateful to Noah, no matter how different our lives offstage may be. But I don't come from the kind of money where I can just buy two tickets to Carnegie Hall like it's nothing. My eyes water with the truth of that. "Well?" he asks, his voice coming from behind me. "How do you feel?" He wraps both of his arms around my waist. I step back into him, taking a deep breath.

"Surreal," I whisper, tearing my eyes away from the auditorium to spin around and look up at him. He gazes down at me, his glasses on the edge of his nose. "I can't believe I'm here. Thank you for this."

"You don't need to thank me," Noah murmurs. "You're here because you have a dream. And you had that dream long before you kissed me."

"I did," I whisper, cupping his face in my hands. The fingers on my left hand scrabble against his cheek the slightest bit, but judging by how he's gazing at me, I doubt he minds. "You're right."

"You belong here." His words send a thrill throughout my entire body. "You belong on this stage."

993 likes

e7string That retarded girl is so lucky someone loves her. Look at how Noah's kissing her cheek. Think Daisy's laughing because she can't fully understand affection? Selfless of Noah to love her so much, right? LOL! Seriously, swipe for video of their first kiss! #naisy

1.7K likes

MaggieNotMary What's he gonna do next? Ask her to prom like all those videos? How sweet! 🏠 👻 #naisy

2.8K likes

VinceViolin Trust retards to not even play the violin correctly. Her chin rest is on the wrong side. #naisy

555 likes

BeauxLikeBow isn't it unprofessional to kiss after a performance, tho? #naisy

JANUARY 9

Amal (10:07 a.m.): Your selfie is so cute! How was your date last night?!

Mazhar (10:08 a.m.): Inquiring minds want to know!

Daisy (10:10 a.m.): It was pretty amazing.

Noah (10:12 a.m.): She's right.

Mazhar (10:13 a.m.): Tell us everything at lunch tomorrow?

Amal (10:14 a.m.) Yes!!! I'll be done babysitting my cousins in Union Square at around 1?

Daisy (10:16 a.m.): Can we split a chocolate pizza?

Amal (10:20 a.m.): You don't even have to ask.

CHAPTER TWENTY-FIVE
DAISY

The next day, Noah, Mazhar, and I head down into the chaos of the Times Square subway station. People stream in every direction as they get on and off the shuttle that goes between here and Grand Central. Since the video, I have noticed some people looking at me a little longer, trying to piece together where they've seen me before. But so far, I have been able to escape any real embarrassing moments.

The busyness—along with the sharp, thick scent of metal and crowds—is welcomed, reminding me that there is some sort of normalcy, that you can still get completely lost in the city.

"Is Amal meeting us at Max Brenner's or at the station?" I ask Mazhar as we near the turnstiles.

"The station." Mazhar smiles at the very thought of seeing his girlfriend.

"All right." I try to smile back at him, stamping down the

feelings that crop up in my stomach as I swipe my MetroCard. *A chocolate pizza is fifteen dollars, which, split between four people, is three dollars and—*

My hip bumps hard into the metal turnstile, bringing me back to the subway station. The crowd of people behind me, jostling to get through, groan and suck their teeth, grumbling about tourists.

As if I needed to feel more awkward, I blink at the blue analog words on the MetroCard reader:

PAID $0.00

BAL $0.00

"Damn it," I whisper.

"What's wrong?" Noah asks as I turn back to him, Mazhar, and the knot of disgruntled New Yorkers behind us.

I hold up my MetroCard, my face hot and blotchy. "My card doesn't have money. I don't know how I forgot; I never let that happen."

Mazhar bites his lip, but Noah gestures at the bulky ticket machines nearby. "A lot has been going on; it makes sense that it slipped your mind. Just go refill it. It's okay. We don't mind waiting." His shoulders almost reach his ears as a coldness manages to seep into my skin, through my winter coat.

"I can't." Stepping to the side and out of people's way, I bend my card in my fist as Mazhar and Noah join me.

"Why not? You should get an unlimited MetroCard. You definitely ride the subway enough to make it worth it," Noah says, holding up his own piece of yellow polyester.

When I don't say anything, Noah's brows knit together, and I shrink a little as I watch him realize what's happening. "Oh, I can refill it for—"

"No." I shake my head, stepping backward. "I can't ask you to do that."

"Okay, well, just let me pay your fare," he says.

I blow out a breath from between my teeth.

"Just for this one ride," he adds. "I have a backup card."

So, I nod, and after swiping Noah's MetroCard through the reader, I nudge past the turnstile, hoping that the promise of chocolate pizza can get rid of this gnawing feeling in my stomach.

• • •

We walk into the honey-colored glow of the restaurant. The smell of pure cocoa surrounds us, and I relax a little.

"Party of four?" the redheaded hostess asks. Mazhar nods. "It'll be about twenty minutes."

Mazhar and Amal smile at us, questions about our date on the tips of their tongues. But before they can ask any of them, a conversation close to the hostess's podium makes my stomach clench.

"Did you see yesterday's episode where Hope Baker sent that terminally ill boy and his entire family to Disney World?" a woman with a short brown bob is saying. "She even flew in his grandparents from Ontario. That woman is such a saint."

"Of course I did," her friend replies, taking off her gloves and putting them in her coat pocket. "But did you see the episode last week with that clip of those musicians?"

"Oh God, yes!" the woman says. "So inspirational, isn't it? I mean, what that poor girl has had to overcome—"

"Evie?" the hostess shouts. "Your table's ready."

The two women head to a table near the bathrooms, and I sigh, closing my eyes.

"Daisy, don't listen to them," Noah tells me bracingly. "They don't know who you are."

"Of course they don't," Mazhar says, crossing his arms. "I know we haven't talked about the meeting you guys had with Principal Loman all that much, but—"

"He can't be serious," Amal hisses. "Having you guys on that show?"

"I thought he was at least going to chew us out because of the kiss." I glance at Noah. We haven't let go of each other's hands since getting on the N train. We haven't talked about the MetroCard situation, either. At least I texted my parents and they're sending me money to refill my card. "But nope. He thought it was cute.

"I get wanting to draw more attention to the academy," I say. "Because more attention and publicity mean more money. And obviously, Principal Loman needed to ask our parents for their permission before even speaking with us about it."

"You don't need to rationalize his horrible behavior," Amal interjects, adjusting her glasses. "You know that, right? I mean, he's basically exploiting you to get the academy more money. Using his star pupils like that? It's absurd."

"Canım." Mazhar touches her shoulder, his eyes soft. "They know."

"But is he really exploiting both of us?" I ask. "All the news reports, that BuzzFeed article Mazhar showed Noah, *The Hope Baker Hour*? They're focused on me. Our duet is only mentioned for a second."

"So it's okay as long as you are the only one being exploited?" Amal takes my free hand in hers. "Daisy, listen to yourself."

"Mazhar?" the hostess finally calls. She takes us up a winding staircase, and the deeper into the restaurant we go, the more people I realize are here. They've all come to shoot chocolate directly into their mouths via syringes or toast marshmallows over miniature firepits—surrounded by blocks of milk, white, and dark chocolate behind glass cases—so we won't be noticed here.

"Is this okay?" The hostess gestures to a yellow booth set against the window overlooking the restaurant's corner of Union Square.

The place around us is loud and buzzing. We order our food and I start to calm down. But the conversation stops when Mazhar curses loudly enough for the couple at a nearby table to look up from their fondue.

"What happened?" I ask, about to bite into my second slice of perfect chocolaty pizza.

Mazhar turns his phone around to face us again. "Principal Loman may not have cared about the kiss," he says, grabbing a napkin to wipe peanut butter sauce and marshmallows from his lips. "But the rest of the internet does."

He scrolls through Instagram, a blur of the same image on dozens of different accounts. Me and Noah, locked together onstage. My hand on his shirt, his hands cupping my face as we kiss.

"But how?" I whisper, looking from Mazhar's phone to him and back again. "The recording stops right before we kiss."

"Someone else must've recorded the kiss." Amal eats the last bit of her crust and grabs her own phone from her bag. "But there's no telling who. It's everywhere. Look." She turns her phone around to face us. "Someone stole your selfie from Carnegie Hall, too. Tons of people are reposting it."

I slump back against the booth, the comments I managed to read burning across my eyes:

So cute!!! #naisy

I LOVE THEM!!! #naisy

Sexy!!! #naisy

Strangers love me and Noah. Strangers started a hashtag for us. Strangers think we're sexy. Strangers . . .

"Wait." I point to Mazhar's phone screen with a slice of pizza. "Go back to that one." I read the caption from a post by a user named e7string, my words shaky and hard at the same time: "'*That retarded girl is so lucky someone loves her.*'"

That word steals the breath from my lungs in a way no other word ever has or can. It's not that I'm unused to hearing it. I've gotten good at ignoring how that word can prick my skin like the roses in Ma's shop. I've had seventeen years of practice.

It's different seeing it written on Instagram than having it be hurled at my face.

The word somehow hurts more because of how casual it looks.

And I can't be here right now.

Tears blur my vision as I edge my way out of the booth, not even bothering to read the rest of the caption aloud. Something about how I'm laughing because I can't understand affection.

"Daisy—" voices say in unison.

I shake my head, my left hand bunched around my coat, my eyes stinging from salt, as I head for the stairs.

"Daisy." My name is heavy in Noah's mouth. I hadn't realized he was following me until now. "You know you're not . . . Please."

I shake my head, wiping away the few tears that have managed to roll down my cheeks. "Please," I repeat. "I just—"

Without finishing my sentence, I walk down the stairs, weave through the knot of people waiting for tables, and emerge onto the street with the word burning a hole in my chest.

CHAPTER TWENTY-SIX
DAISY

I end up on the Strand's second floor, grateful that the bookstore's towering shelves and narrow aisles shield me from the rest of the world.

Somehow its YA contemporary section is blessedly empty, so I've been sitting behind a set of rolling stairs. For how long, I'm not sure. Long enough to stop crying, at least. The tears on my cheeks are drying just in time to hear footsteps approaching. I can tell they're Noah's just by the sound.

"Hi." His voice creaks like the old wood floor beneath his shoes. "Can I sit with you?"

I look up, gazing at him through the slats between the steps I'm hiding behind. "I think your legs might be too long. It won't be comfortable."

"I'll manage." Noah sidesteps past a row of books and folds his legs to his chest to sit beside me. His body is warm against mine, and still smelling like cocoa.

Neither of us says anything. We're in one of the world's most famous bookstores, surrounded by words, and we can't come up with any ourselves.

"How'd you find me?" I finally ask.

"Amal and Mazhar figured this is where you would come," Noah replies. "They're in the manga section."

"Did they send you?" I ask. A creak of footsteps fills the beat of silence.

"No." Noah offers me his hand, and I thread my fingers through his. His calluses still feel the same. Rough, but calming. "I asked them to give us a moment, though. I wanted to be the one to find you. They do this kind of thing for each other all the time."

I'm reminded of the depressive episode Mazhar had in tenth grade before he was diagnosed and got on medication. He and Amal had been together for two years. Amal was the only person who could get him out of bed and get him to eat a full meal. She was at his apartment every morning to eat breakfast and take him to school until he started seeing Dr. Singh.

Now Noah's here for me.

Noah takes a deeper breath, his fingers shivering against mine. "I have no idea what I can say to make what happened okay."

"Because there isn't anything." I sigh, closing my eyes against a fresh batch of tears.

Every microaggression, every well-meaning comment, every slur.

There isn't anything that can make the pain of those just disappear.

Noah moves closer to me. The heat of his leg spreads warmth through my body. Like electrotherapy, that same pulse of electricity. I crave it, needing more of it instead of wanting it to be over.

I never want Noah to stop touching me.

"If you want." His fingers trickle down until they're threaded through mine on my right hand. The insides of our wrists touch and my heart races from behind the safety of my ribs. "I can distract you."

"Please?" I don't want to think about Instagram, or that comment, or that word that's been burned behind my eyes. I don't want to think about how there are probably hundreds of other comments like that one. I don't want to think about *The Hope Baker Hour.*

I just want to be with this boy sitting beside me, in this bookstore where we are somehow still alone. His heart beats in time with mine as we kiss, taking turns pressing each other's backs to book spines behind us. His tongue explores mine, sending shivers down my arm that transition into muscle spasms.

"Thank you," I whisper to him.

"You're welcome." He kisses my forehead, scuttling back against a collection of books with blue spines. I hear Mazhar and Amal and remember they are in the section behind these shelves.

Our friends' eyes gleam as they grin at our flushed faces, messy hair, and swollen lips. "Ah, making out in a bookstore." Mazhar sighs, pressing the back of his hand to his forehead. "It's like a scene out of a Hallmark movie." He holds up two plastic bags in his other hand. "I took our leftover pizza to go. We can't let it go to waste. My apartment?"

When we take the Q back to Mazhar's apartment, we don't even heat up our pizza. We just eat it cold, watching anime until Mazhar and Amal go to perform wudu, then their afternoon prayer.

This normalcy—being with my friends, our bellies full of chocolate—I needed just as much as that kiss.

CHAPTER TWENTY-SEVEN
DAISY

"Can you sue them?" Nonna dumps more spaghetti than I'll ever be able to realistically eat onto my plate. Sauce night—my grandparents' entire place filled with the scent of garlic, onions, basil, and tomatoes—is more sacred than church.

It didn't keep me nearly as distracted as what happened in the bookstore, but it helped. Until I had to tell my family about the Instagram comment.

"No one's suing anyone, Ma." Dad looks up from pulverizing a meatball for Holly, whose face is already stained red.

"Sal, let the girl make her own damn decisions," Nonno grumbles. "Arthur Donati downstairs used to be a lawyer, you know. We could—"

"I'm not suing anyone," I say, spreading a ladleful of sauce over my pasta. I grab the container of fresh Parmesan and sprinkle on way too much.

"If only there was some kind of technology that sent those comments to their parents," Nonna hisses. "They'd be too ashamed to say anything, then."

"You're retired," Ma points out, smiling at her. "Become an app developer."

"Maybe I will." Nonna places a large basket of garlic bread in the center of the table hard enough for the ice in our glasses to clink. We join hands, and she leads us in saying grace before we start eating.

For a while it's just the sound of forks scraping on plates and the crunch of garlic bread. Ma is smiling, but it doesn't reach her eyes, so I know what's coming.

"Are we going to talk about Hope Baker inviting you and Noah on her show, sweetheart?" she asks.

My fork clatters against the plate, and I take longer than needed to wipe my lips, but before I can speak, Nonno jumps in. "Hope Baker gets to sit with you and your boyfriend before we do? Daisy, that's not right."

"The holidays are a busy time," I point out, my face probably close to the same color as the sauce. "And besides, she . . ." I close my eyes, thinking of how *The Hope Baker Hour*'s set always looks. Its silver furniture, its fake New York City skyline, its overly perky host.

I feel Ma's hand cover mine. It's rough from the flower shop, but still warm. I open my eyes, surprised by the touch. Instinctively I look over and see Ma's other hand is on Holly's shoulder.

"Daisy and Noah don't have to appear on the show," she tells the table. "It's their decision. And," she adds before Nonno can jump in, "we'll just have to invite Noah and his family over for dinner soon."

"We'll have sauce," Nonna declares, plucking another piece of garlic bread from the basket. "But"—she looks over at me again—"going on the show is worth thinking about, you know. It could lead to wonderful things for you and Noah. Did you see last week's episode about how she surprised an entire family with a trip to Disney World?"

•   •   •

Later that night, I'm just barely asleep when I hear voices hissing down the hall. I open my eyes, blinking against the darkness shot through with constant city light from my window. I immediately look at Holly's toddler bed. She's curled up, her pudgy arms coiled around her stuffed pink octopus, her little snores filling the room the way traffic fills the streets.

I pull off my quilt and tiptoe over to the door, easing it open.

"Sal, you know we can't *make* her do anything," Ma is saying. I think they're in the kitchen; the creak of Nonna's old chairs gives it away. "You've seen the news; you've read the articles. They think she—you know how cruel people can be."

"I know." Dad pauses to drink something. I realized when Holly was born, not as prematurely as I was, but still enough to warrant time in the NICU, that they always drink coffee when they talk at night. "Daisy isn't special because of her cerebral palsy. But the *world* thinks she is."

"And does our daughter need that pressure?" Ma hisses. "Ask yourself that."

"Of course she doesn't, Ottavia," Dad says. "But you also know where she's headed."

"Juilliard."

A painful silence, one that pounds in my head, stretches between them. Anyone should be happy when they hear their parents talk about their future. I can't ignore the kaleidoscope of butterflies that swarm in my stomach.

But I also know why they're bringing it up.

"We're still paying off hospital bills from Holly's birth," Dad continues in a hushed voice, as though he'd rather not think about it. "And before she was born, by the grace of God, we . . . Ottavia, we don't have the money to send our daughters to college. My parents will give what they've set aside, but it's not nearly enough for what Daisy will need. What she deserves."

Ma's still quiet. I hear her swallow her own sip of coffee, and I mimic her, tasting salt from the tears streaming down my cheeks. "She's worked so hard to get into Juilliard," she murmurs with cracks in her voice.

"Yes." Dad sighs. "Ottavia, I'm only thinking about our daughter's best interest. I don't want her to lose her dream just because we can't afford it. I already feel like I'm letting her down."

Daisy (1:03 a.m.): Hi. Are you awake?

Noah (1:03 a.m.): I am now. Are you okay?

Daisy (1:05 a.m.): Let's go on The Hope Baker Hour. It could pay for Juilliard.

CHAPTER TWENTY-EIGHT
NOAH

"We have a problem," I tell Dr. Singh instead of saying hello when I sit down in his office at our next session.

Dr. Singh looks up from his tablet, his eyebrows raised, his stylus poised between his fingers. "What's wrong?"

"Um." I pause, unsure about how to explain the madness of the internet, particularly when it revolves around me and Daisy.

So, I tell him: Our duet is now approaching five million views. New articles are being published every day, spinning a love story that no one actually knows but everyone loves to tell. New Instagram, Facebook, and Twitter posts are popping up practically every minute, all with #naisy. Which sounds like the name of some new allergy medication instead of a hashtag about my and Daisy's relationship.

"And now," I continue, my throat hurting from talking so

much, "our appearance on *The Hope Baker Hour* is being filmed January fourteenth."

"But you were both initially reluctant to do this when your principal proposed the idea," Dr. Singh clarifies. I nod. "Why the change?"

"Daisy—" I swallow, reaching for my hair but pulling down my hands. I've realized that I play with my hair when I'm anxious, so I'm trying to stop. "Daisy said it could pay for Juilliard. Apparently, *The Hope Baker Hour* gives money away every show."

Dr. Singh readjusts himself in his chair. "And you both want to attend Juilliard?"

"Yes."

"So, what's the problem with that?" he asks. "Is it the way in which you'd be getting the money? You don't want to be put up in front of an audience?"

"No." I shake my head, focusing on the wall of windows behind him. Central Park is covered in a thin layer of snow, the tops of the skeletal trees lined with it. "We're musicians; an audience isn't the problem." Dr. Singh waits, letting me be ready to finish. "It's just that it doesn't seem like she actually wants to do this. I'm worried that she's pretending to be okay with all this because it means she can go to Juilliard. I—I'm not going to say no. She can't possibly afford Juilliard without this money and that's just not an obstacle for me. God, I sound like an *ass*. I just don't want her to be exploited."

"You're regretting having agreed," Dr. Singh says.

"Yes." I rub my chest where the word seems to poke at it. "I don't want Daisy to feel like she *has* to do this."

"Worrying about her is understandable, as she's your girlfriend," my psychiatrist points out. "Now, you mentioned that you think the money is what changed Daisy's mind. Is the idea of that uncomfortable to you?"

"No." I shake my head. "I mean, yes. Um." My eyes widen behind my glasses. "I'm sorry."

Dr. Singh waves his hand. "Continue."

"Well." I feel like I have a stone lodged behind my Adam's apple. "I don't need the money." The sour taste of bile fills my mouth as I realize how horrible, how entitled, I sound. "My parents can afford to send me to Juilliard. They paid for Douglas to attend when he got accepted. They also paid for Gavin to attend the Royal Conservatoire of Scotland. They'll pay for me. But Daisy . . ." My voice trails off, grimacing. "Her family doesn't have money like mine."

Dr. Singh lets a beat of silence pass between us. "Daisy could benefit from a scholarship."

"She would *need* a scholarship," I say, nodding.

"And that makes you uncomfortable?" I nod again, not trusting myself to speak. "Do you recognize how faulty that thinking is? Most college students require financial aid and scholarships. I'm not trying to patronize you or anything, Noah. I'm just doing my job as your psychiatrist to talk through things that may be troubling you."

"I know." I clear my throat, and it's like I'm dislodging glass. "But before Daisy, I barely knew how to communicate with anyone, period. What should I do?"

"What do you think you should do?" Dr. Singh asks, sitting back in his chair.

"I always thought that was a stereotype," I respond, smiling a little. "In the movies when the therapists flip their patient's questions back at them."

"This is a place for you to get to the bottom of what you are thinking and feeling," Dr. Singh says, smiling at me. "I can't tell you what you should do; only you can really know that."

"But I don't think I know how to handle this one."

"Well, it's not every day you're invited on one of New York's biggest talk shows because of a viral video millions of people around the world have seen. It's bound to bring some anxiety and raise some questions."

"But I'm not anxious about the show. I'm worried about Daisy." Dr. Singh raises his eyebrows like I've finally gotten to the thing he already knew.

"You know, Noah . . ." He takes a deep breath, like he's trying to find the kindest way to say what's coming next. "It's lovely that you care this deeply about Daisy. But you can't always know exactly what she wants or what she's feeling. Maybe this is a choice she has to make for herself."

"But what if she's making the wrong choice?" I ask, panic taking root in my chest.

"With all due respect, you aren't in Daisy's shoes. You can't know, with certainty, what the right choice for her is. Maybe you go on the show and she feels exploited and regrets it. Maybe you don't go on the show and she regrets it later when she can't go to Juilliard. Either choice might cause her some grief, and you can't keep her from those hard experiences."

"Well." My thoughts are starting to race a bit, and my hand starts to make its way up to my hair. I take a deep breath, close my eyes, and lower my hand. "What can I do, then? For her?"

"I think you know," he says, his voice soft and kind.

"Be there for her," I say, letting my hands run through my hair anyway.

Dr. Singh glances at the time on his wall clock. Our session must almost be over. "Let's talk about your medicine," he says. "Given the effects you're experiencing on this medication, I'm going to suggest you try a new one, okay? Remember we talked about how we might have to try a few different things before landing on the right one? Let's try and find you something that doesn't make you feel so tired all the time."

I nod.

"Now, before we can do anything, we need to wean you off your current one over the course of a few weeks, where you'll slowly stop taking it. We'll revisit that after your next session, okay?"

"Sure," I say, suddenly remembering why I'm in therapy.

CHAPTER TWENTY-NINE
DAISY

On the day of our appearance on *The Hope Baker Hour*, I'm convinced that my heart has been replaced by a hummingbird. Its wings beat rapidly in my chest. We ran through a rehearsal this morning, but it didn't calm my nerves.

Noah and I have been watching the show on the massive flat-screen TV in the greenroom. A producer as perky as Hope Baker herself ("Call me Melody! It's so nice to meet you! My daughters, both in band at their school, you know, can't stop talking about you two!") brought us here before showtime, wishing us luck.

"Are you okay?" I pause about halfway across the room. It's all silvery walls, glittery tile, chilled bottles of fancy mineral water, and a white sofa Noah is sitting on. His spine is flush with the couch and his shoulders are straight, as if he appears on talk shows for fun.

"No." I pull my rigid left arm down with my right hand, willing myself not to cry. We had our hair and makeup done, and I don't want to mess it up. "How are you so calm?" I ask.

Noah gets to his feet in one fluid motion, taking both of my hands in his. "I'm not." His face flushes, adding a pop of color to his deep navy dress shirt and black slacks that match my dress and tights. We were advised to wear color-coordinated outfits, the way we do onstage. The way we did in the video of the duet.

"Why haven't you said anything?" I murmur, wrapping my arms around his waist. My fingers lightly skim his leather belt.

Noah pulls me closer and kisses my lips. "Because." I feel his breath against my mouth as he speaks. "We have more than one thing to worry about right now."

For a moment, I had forgotten about Juilliard.

• • •

"My next guests performed a duet for their school that went viral," Hope Baker says, her voice slightly muffled by the tall silver doors Noah and I are standing behind. We immediately grip each other's hands, which Melody encouraged.

"Since then," Hope continues, "they've captured the hearts of not only New York City but the rest of the world as well with their inspiring love story. Please welcome Daisy Abano and Noah Moray!"

The doors slide open like an elevator's. Melody gives us the signal to walk out onstage. A cheesy pop song blasts from unseen speakers as the audience cheers. Hope stands up and invites us to sit with her on a silver love seat I'm positive wasn't there before.

They wanted Noah and me to sit next to each other to make us seem cuter, make our relationship easier for the internet to fawn over.

I can't look at Noah, but I know from the way he tightens his fingers around mine that he's thinking the same thing.

"Wow!" Hope breathes as we all sit back down, the music cutting off. "Daisy, Noah, it's so nice to have you on the show."

"Thank you," we say in unison, which earns an "aww" from the crowd.

"Of course!" I'm confident Hope Baker can only go so long without ending a sentence with an exclamation point. "Now the whole world knows about you two." Her set's backdrop of the New York City skyline fades away, revealing a still from our duet video: us, frozen, mid-performance. "Daisy." Her hazel eyes cut to me, shimmering beneath the too-hot stage lights. "Let's jump right in. How does it feel to be such an inspiration to so many people?"

Don't say anything that the world doesn't want to hear, I remind myself. *Don't.*

"Well," I begin, my tongue sticking to my top teeth a little, "I'm not. I'm a musician."

"You can be both, definitely." Hope nods, her smile never flinching. "You can't deny the impact you're having. Being a violist is a feat, even when one isn't differently abled."

Sour bile crawls up my throat, but I swallow it.

"She's a violinist," Noah corrects her softly. My eyes flit to him. He's sitting up straighter than I ever could, smiling at Hope despite squeezing my hand. "Easy mistake. But they're completely different instruments, even if their names sound similar."

"My apologies," Hope says airily. "And you're a cellist, right, Noah?" He nods, and she leans forward, her yellow gingham shirt not even so much as rumpling. "Can you tell me," she says, redirecting the conversation, "what it's been like to go viral, then?"

"It's been overwhelming," Noah admits, gesturing to both of us. "As musicians, we're used to being onstage; we're used to having people watching us. We've been playing for years, and we hope to attend performing arts conservatories next year, but we've never had anything like this happen to us before."

"You both want to go to Juilliard, is that right?" she asks. "The top-rated music school in the world."

"Yes," we say in unison again, earning applause from the crowd this time. We glance at each other, and our eyes soften. "Together."

The crowd becomes a mess of squeals and cheering, which Hope practically feeds off. "Well," she says, beaming, "I think we have something that can help with that." Hope pauses, shimmying in her massive chair across from us. "Here on *The Hope Baker Hour*, we believe in rewarding those who do good in the world. So, it's my pleasure to personally present you both with checks for fifty thousand dollars!"

That's the entire first year's tuition.

My mouth falls open, but no sound comes out. I'm not sure what's worse: that I can feel the color spilling across my face and down my neck, or that I can hear my mom's muffled sobs through the audience's eruption.

Two producers rush onstage, handing us comically large checks addressed to me and Noah, signed by Hope Baker with a flourish.

"Congratulations!" Hope sings. "We're going to take a break, but we'll be right back with more from Daisy and Noah!"

The same cotton-candy pop music from before plays us out and Hope is ushered backstage, leaving me and Noah on set, clutching both each other and the checks. Melody rushes over to remove our mics in case we want to stretch our legs or use the bathroom, then leaves us alone.

"Oh my God," I whisper. "Noah, this isn't happening."

"It already did," he whispers back, glancing out into the audience, where our families are all seated in the front row. "Are you okay?"

I lean into his shoulder, and his arm goes around my waist. "You've asked me that already."

"I know," he murmurs. "But that was before we were actually on a talk show." I make the mistake of looking out into the audience, where people are pointing and smiling at us, their heads tilted to the side in that condescending way. "Before I was reminded how the rest of the world sees me," I mumble.

"That's not how I see you. I promise." Noah presses his lips to my forehead, going quiet.

"What are you thinking about?" I ask when he pulls away.

"Um." Noah's hand is in his hair. He leans as close to me as he can. "Daisy, what if I—Daisy, what if I gave you my check?"

His question is a whisper. But it's like he shouted it for the entire studio to hear. A coldness races down my spine and along my arms until my left hand is coiled in a muscle spasm against his shoulder.

I open my mouth, but words won't come out. Just the faintest stream of air that lets me know my throat is still working.

Who doesn't need an extra fifty thousand dollars? A person who lives in a penthouse, obviously. I can see the articles and social media posts now: PRODIGY CELLIST GIVES LESS FORTUNATE GIRLFRIEND MASSIVE CHECK.

Like it's nothing. Because to Noah, it's in the same realm as unlimited MetroCards and tickets to Carnegie Hall.

"Daisy?" he prods. "My parents are already prepared to send me to Juilliard. I can just give you the money."

"Don't be ridiculous," I murmur. My eyes don't meet his. "You keep it."

We're given word that we're going to start filming again and Hope Baker rejoins us onstage. Her makeup has been touched up; her smile looks like it still hasn't moved.

"Ready?" she asks cheerily before we begin rolling again.

"And we're back with Daisy Abano and Noah Moray, two musicians who went viral after their amazing performance," Hope says. "We just rewarded them with checks for fifty thousand dollars each, so how are you feeling right now?"

"Incredible," we say.

"Thank you so much," I tell her. "This will obviously be a big help."

"Just as you've helped so many people, Daisy," Hope simpers. "By overcoming your cerebral palsy, I think you've reminded everyone that anything is possible as long as one is determined enough to prove themselves. You are disabled, but you still became a violinist."

Not but. *My strings are reversed. My chin rest is on the right side. I am disabled* and *I am a violinist. I'm not overcoming anything*, I want to say.

But after what happened in the first segment, I don't trust myself to speak.

"Hope?" Noah asks, polite and composed as he's been this entire time. "Can I say something, please?"

"Certainly." Hope grins, nodding at him.

"Thank you." Noah clears his throat, but it's a dry sound. His fingers are shaking against mine. "The world is focusing on Daisy's disability," he continues. "That's all they're seeing." He stares at her. "That's all that you're seeing, too. But I'm her boyfriend, and I don't see Daisy as disabled."

It's like I've plunged into the snow outside. Chills race down my spine, spreading along my arms and legs, until my muscles are too tight to move.

"Excuse me?" I know I should keep quiet since we're on TV, but the words are out before I can stop them. And they keep rushing, like I'm making up for keeping quiet minutes ago. "How could you say you don't see me as being disabled? That would be like me saying I don't see that you carry your cello around like it's your firstborn child." His mouth falls open a little. "It's *ridiculous*. It's *insulting*. My disability is *here*, Noah. It's right in front of you." I jerkily raise our joined hands between us. He's been holding my left hand this entire time. "It's a part of me. And there's nothing wrong with that."

I don't wait for Noah to react before I get to my feet and pull my hand from his, letting it hover at my hip, not bothering to put it down. "I need a few minutes." The silence from the audience presses against my ears.

"Daisy," Hope interjects, her perkiness breaking just a bit. "How about you sit back down, okay? We haven't even discussed your love story yet. Maybe talking—"

I remove my lapel mic and walk offstage, through the doors, down the hall, and past producers whose calls fall on the edges of my ears. They can edit around us. Stop at the part where Noah and I were given the money, make themselves look as generous as possible.

Noah is right behind me, but I don't look at him until we're in the lobby of the studio. It's surrounded by floor-to-ceiling windows, letting Times Square spill inside. Pink and yellow lights from a screen advertising the M&M's store splash across the shiny marble floor.

"Daisy." My name sounds like breaking glass in his mouth. "What was that?"

A muscle spasm slithers down my left arm, making me bunch my hand into a fist. "You don't realize what you just did," I whisper. "At all. Do you?"

"You've *seen* the internet," Noah hisses, cramming his hand into his hair. "You heard what Hope said, too. All the world is focusing on is the fact that you're so inspiring for having cerebral palsy and still achieving orchestral success. I was *protecting* you."

"By completely ignoring who I am?" I glare at him, my throat hurting as I raise my voice. "*That's* your solution? Convincing the internet to see past my disability to get them to leave me alone? Did it ever occur to you that maybe I don't *need* protection or— or your *money*?" I spit out the last word.

Noah's eyes go dark behind his glasses; his jaw becomes set. "What's that supposed to mean?"

"You know exactly what!" My words feel like they're going to pierce my skin. "Taking me to Carnegie Hall was one thing—"

"We were on a date," Noah snaps. "If it made you uncomfortable—"

"But offering me your check?!" I plow on. Saliva pools in

my mouth and for one second, I'm terrified I'm going to collapse and start sobbing. "I—I don't even want Hope's money! Noah, why would you think I want yours?" I hug my tight arms to my chest. "Tell me."

"Because I . . ." He puts his hand over his mouth, like he's trying to keep the words inside.

"Tell me."

"You need the money more than I do." He says this as if it's not the very thing that makes us so different.

"No." I shake my head, hoping to dislodge the truth of his words from between my ears. "What I *need* is for the rest of the world to wake up and *respect* me. To see me as fully human, something my own boyfriend is apparently incapable of!"

"Daisy," he whispers, color draining from his face. "I didn't mean—"

"Yes, you did." Tears are damming up behind my eyes. "Even if you don't realize it. You said you don't see me the way other people do, that you don't see me as disabled." My voice hitches painfully in my throat. "And while that's a step above how the world sees me right now, *you* aren't seeing my disability as a part of who I am. Even if you don't think of it as something for me to overcome or as a burden, you're not respecting me.

"I trusted you." My voice is nothing more than the scrape of an untreated bow too near the bridge, a mistake that an amateur makes. "Noah, I *trusted* that you saw all of me."

"I do," he pleads. "I—I *see* you."

I shake my head, walking backward until I hit the glass windows. The coldness seeps into my skin through my dress. "No." Damp eyelashes brush against my cheeks. "You don't." I take a deep breath, ignoring how my heart has leapt up into my throat. "So, I can't—I can't do this. Not anymore."

"Daisy." He's looking up at me now, but his eyes are staring through me instead. They're gleaming with tears, same as mine, a duet neither of us rehearsed but have somehow played perfectly. "I'm *sorry*. Please don't do this."

Instead of answering, I push away from the window and disappear into Times Square, leaving Noah behind.

FROM: Joel Liebowitz <joel.liebowitz@juilliard.edu>
TO: Daisy Abano <daisy.abano@mamp.edu>
DATE: January 14, 12:00 p.m.
SUBJECT: Congratulations! You've Been Invited to a Live Audition!

Dear Daisy,
Congratulations! On behalf of our faculty and staff, I am pleased to invite you to a live audition at the Juilliard School in New York City. Your audition date is Wednesday, March 3, at 1:15 p.m. Please be sure to prepare your live audition repertoire in advance, the components for which are available on our website.
Sincerely,
Joel Liebowitz
President
The Juilliard School

JANUARY 14

Mazhar (12:30 p.m.): Did you get your email?! 😮 😮

Daisy (12:55 p.m.): Yeah. I got invited for a live audition.

Amal (12:55 p.m.): YAY!!! DAISY, CONGRATULATIONS! 🐱

Mazhar (12:55 p.m.): CONGRATULATIONS!!!!!!!! 🐱

Daisy (12:56 p.m.): But I broke up with Noah.

JANUARY 15

Noah (11:08 a.m.): Amal?

Amal (11:09 a.m.): Are you okay?

Noah (11:11 a.m.): No. I have a headache from switching medications.

Noah (11:11 a.m.): But that isn't entirely why I'm not okay.

Amal (11:12 a.m.): I know.

Noah (11:14 a.m.): Can I come practice for my audition, please?

Amal (11:15 a.m.): Yes.

CHAPTER THIRTY
NOAH

Dr. Singh calls me into his office for our monthly session. I wave, but his eyes don't linger on my bandaged fingers. They aren't broken calluses this time; instead they're actual cuts along my string hand from how hard I've been practicing. Yesterday, I actually stopped when it started to hurt instead of pushing myself. My dad helped me bandage my hand and reminded me that playing perfectly can't fix being broken up with.

When I got to Amal's apartment afterward, she took one look at my bandaged hand, told me to leave my cello in her bedroom, and declared that we'd be watching anime instead.

It takes me ten minutes to even say a word, but eventually, I explain everything.

"Well, I'm proud of you for stopping," Dr. Singh commends me. "That's progress, Noah. As for your breakup with Daisy, it sounds to me like you underestimated how strong-willed she can be in herself."

"I know," I murmur.

"I know it's still pretty new," Dr. Singh says. "But how has your new medication been so far?"

"Good." I nod, realizing the truth beyond the word. "I haven't had any anxiety attacks, and I haven't been overly sleepy like with the other one. Given all that has happened, I guess it has been working really well."

"As odd and as uncomfortable as these situations can be," Dr. Singh begins, "be proud of your improvements, okay?"

I nod, my eyes drifting to his office windows.

Today the sky outside is a perfect, bright blue. Not a cloud in sight.

But in my head?

There's a fog too opaque for me to see through.

CHAPTER THIRTY-ONE

DAISY

It's been three weeks since I received my invitation to a Juilliard live audition.

It's also been three weeks since I broke up with Noah in the middle of Times Square Broadcast Studios.

You would think that getting to the next step of the Juilliard admissions process would help distract me from the breakup. But it doesn't, because I know without even texting him that Noah got the same email. He's auditioning, too. I can tell from watching him during orchestra practice. How he curls around his cello, stiffer than he's been these past few months. How he doesn't look up from his music stand. How his hands are wrapped in bandages most of the time. How when the bell rings for the period to end, he packs up without talking to anyone and makes his way to our next class, like he doesn't even notice the students around him.

The fact that we can't talk about our auditions hurts just as much as missing him does.

But I can't be with someone who's willing to ignore a part of me.

At least we don't have to worry about our episode of *The Hope Baker Hour* airing for another week.

"Are you okay?" Mazhar's question brings me back to the Q train.

School just ended. Usually, Mazhar and I would be going to his apartment to practice for our live auditions, like we have these last few weeks. But today, we're heading to Amal's apartment. She and Mazhar are leaving for California tomorrow to tour the San Francisco Conservatory of Music and the San Francisco Art Institute. Mazhar has his own live audition to attend.

"Yeah," I lie. "I'm just thinking about my audition." A slow and fast movement from a nineteenth-, twentieth-, and twenty-first-century concerto, two movements from a Bach sonata or partita, a Paganini caprice, and a brilliant concert piece.

"That's not what he meant," Amal murmurs, glancing at her boyfriend. "Are you okay since the breakup?"

"You haven't really talked about it," Mazhar adds, gesturing between us. "And I get why. Our auditions are keeping us busy. But it must be hard for you, not being with Noah anymore?"

"We know you had your reasons, but still. Breaking up with someone you love must be hard," Amal adds.

Love? I stumble into the pole at her words. *I'm in love with Noah?*

"How—" I try.

"The winter semiformal," Amal continues. "You were in love with him then."

The dancing. The spinning. The laughter. How his hands felt in mine. How his voice felt in my ears.

Oh God. My heart leaps up into my throat. *Of course.*

"That's why it hurts so much," I murmur.

"So, the question is, Daisy"—Mazhar readjusts his hand on the pole—"what are you going to do about it?"

·   ·   ·

Amal is debating between her floral-patterned skirts when the doorbell rings, echoing through the apartment and down the hall.

"Ali!" Amal sings, studying her magenta skirt with bright yellow hibiscus flowers. "Can you get the door, please?"

"Why don't you get it?" her younger brother answers immediately over the sounds of *Mario Kart* from the living room. "I'm busy!"

"You can pause your race," Amal fires back. "*I'm* the one flying across the country tomorrow! Besides, you're closer to the door."

"Fine!"

Ali shuffles across the carpet and opens the door, his next words sending a bucket of ice down my spine: "Hey, Noah." My head snaps up at the sound of his name. "Amal!" Ali calls down the hall. "Noah's here again!"

They walk down the hall, and when they reach Amal's room, my entire body tenses up from my place on her bed, the paisley duvet cover beneath me suddenly seeming both itchy and hot. Whether it's from muscle spasms, the fact that I'm in love with Noah, or seeing him just casually in Amal's apartment, I'm not sure.

It's probably a combination of the three.

"What are you doing here?" we ask in unison, staring at each other. I know our friends are looking back and forth between us, our conversation on the train replaying in their minds.

"You don't even live here, Daisy," Noah says, his words shivering on the word *live*. "Last time I checked, this was the Upper East Side, not Brooklyn."

"I know where I live," I snap, surprised by his tone. "And I know where you live, too, Noah. Amal is my best friend, and she's leaving tomorrow. Of course I came. Why don't you go back to your penthouse?"

"Hey," Amal says reproachfully. "He can be here if he wants." The end of her sentence hangs in the air, like there's more she wants to say but is keeping it to herself. I focus on a few of the canvases Amal has hung up on her walls: the Union Square Greenmarket, a sunset on a beach in Karachi, even a selfie of her and Mazhar re-created with individual dots of paint.

"By that logic, so can Daisy," Mazhar points out softly, glancing at Amal.

"She's my friend, too," Noah adds, almost mumbling the words. I immediately feel bad. "They both are. I wanted to say goodbye."

I can feel our friends' eyes on us like the heat of the sun beyond Amal's bedroom window.

"Daisy?" Mazhar says at the same time Amal says, "Noah?"

I look up at them. Mazhar's holding Amal's hand. Her eyes are soft behind a pair of sparkly fuchsia frames.

"Have you talked to each other?" Amal begins.

"At all?" Mazhar continues. "Since you broke up?"

Their words lie heavily in the air between us, settling somewhere uncomfortably in my chest.

"Look." Noah's gaze finally shifts from me to Mazhar, then finally to Amal. "I'm sorry. I'm just going to leave."

"Me too." Tears prick at my eyes. "This is supposed to be exciting for you guys."

"We're ruining it," Noah mutters. "Have a good trip. Amal, text me when you land, okay?" he adds before exiting her bedroom, the snap of the apartment door coming soon after.

Amal nods at his question, as if he were still here to see it.

"Sorry." I speak to Amal's neatly folded prayer rug in the corner of her room, unable to meet my friends' eyes.

When I reach the hallway, my violin case bouncing sharply on my shoulder, I nearly walk into Noah, who's gazing behind me.

"You've been coming here," I say. "Since we broke up. Haven't you?"

Noah nods, shutting his eyes. Now that we're the closest we've been in weeks, I can see the pale purple circles have come back beneath them. "When you . . ." His voice trails off. "When you broke up with me, I had to talk to someone."

"Because you couldn't talk to me." I ball my hands into fists at my sides, the tiny bites of my fingernails against my palms keeping me from crying.

"Exactly," Noah says. "I just started a new medication, too." I step back. He didn't have to tell me, but there's a comfort to it, for both of us. "It's okay, but it's been an adjustment. Amal has been a really great friend."

"She's good at that." I smile just a little. "Um. What else have you been doing?"

"I've just been rehearsing for my audition," he continues, his cheeks pink. "Rehearsing like I always used to, longer than I should. I've seen the sunrise a lot. I come here because Amal keeps me in check, reminds me when it's time to stop. Now . . ."

"She's leaving," I finish. "Mazhar, too. I've been rehearsing at his apartment. It's been nice, since my parents can't stop talking about this miracle sent through Hope Baker." My back straightens as soon as it comes out. I didn't mean to bring it up. The money. That day.

"So, I guess neither of us will have them to distract us now."

Noah tries to take the conversation back a few steps, his Adam's apple bobbing sharply in his throat.

"Yeah," I whisper. "I guess not."

Before he can say anything else, I pivot on my heel, disappearing into the elevator, trying not to think about how much I wanted to reach out and touch him.

I'm in love with you, I want to say as the doors slide shut in front of me. *And I don't know what to do about it.*

CHAPTER THIRTY-TWO
NOAH

After school on Monday, I take off my shoes and am halfway down the hallway when my dad steps in front of me.

"Put your cello away and your shoes back on," he says. "We're taking Haggis on a walk."

Upon hearing one of his favorite words, Haggis rockets from the living room, barking and spinning between our legs.

"Why?" I ask over our dog's excited yapping. "I have to rehearse."

"Not when you haven't been outside since Scotland," Dad points out cheerily. I open my mouth to protest, but he continues. "I'll get Haggis ready to go. C'mon, then."

By the time I carry my cello to our practice room and retie my shoes, Dad already has Haggis in one of his tweed coats and clipped to the end of his leash. He waits until we're outside and a block away from our apartment before saying anything.

"So," he begins. "How are you doin'?"

"Fine," I supply, shrugging. "I have my songs down. Now it's just—"

"I'm not talking about music." He waves the hand not holding Haggis's leash, placing his pointer finger directly above the bridge of my glasses. "I'm talking about you, Noah," he clarifies, dropping his hand. "How are you doin' since the breakup?"

"What would you know about it?" I ask instead of answering him. "You and Mom have this amazing, perfect relationship."

To my surprise, Dad laughs, the deep sound making the hairs on the back of my neck stand up. "That's what you think, eh?" he asks. "Nearly thirty-one years married and no problems at all?"

Haggis stops at a tree to raise his leg and pee.

"Well." I swallow hard around the lump in my throat. "You are in love, aren't you?"

"Of course we are," Dad murmurs. The sidewalk crunches under our feet, Haggis's claws clicking against the concrete. "Your mum is the most important woman in the world to me. But I'm not on this walk to talk about us right now." He looks over at me. "Are *you* okay? We've been worried."

I blink, shrugging. "Yeah, I'm fine."

"So 'fine' includes your fingers bleeding from practice?" Dad raises his bushy eyebrows. He had to help me bandage them again over the weekend. I still feel the hydrogen peroxide tingling on my skin.

"Not exactly." I shrug, my shoulders reaching my ears. "But I need to nail this Juilliard audition."

"Not at the expense of your hands," Dad tells me. "Your music is obviously important and of course we want you to do well and get accepted. But we want you to be careful, too."

"When I'm playing music, I'm not focused on Daisy." I blurt out the truth that's been burning a hole through my heart for the last few weeks. Which seems ridiculous since it wasn't that long ago when she and music were inextricably linked. "She's on my mind all the time. But it's like if I can perfect my repertoire, then I don't need to think about the problems we had. At least there is one thing I can fix."

Dad sighs, gazing up at the bright winter sun. "Let me tell you a story."

"A story?" We stop at a crosswalk, waiting for the walk signal. I look at him. His cheeks are ruddy beneath his beard.

"You don't know this, but your mum was already three months pregnant with Douglas when we got married."

I trip over the curb, but Dad catches my arm, keeping me on my feet. "Excuse me?"

"The night she told me, I only knew a few things," Dad continues as we walk across the street. "One, I was due to return home in a few weeks. Two, your mum's family is Irish Catholic. She lied about where she was at night. Back then, if they knew she was havin' sex before marriage, let alone the fact that she got pregnant? They probably would've disowned her."

"And you didn't want to leave," I fill in, a chill racing down my spine that has nothing to do with the frigid February wind whipping my hair. "Obviously."

"I didn't come to America to fall in love or start a family," Dad says. "But both of those things happened. So, I proposed, and we got married." He holds up his left hand, displaying his worn-out gold wedding band, the same kind that Mom has. "We didn't have time or money to get fancy rings, so we settled for what we could afford. Even now, your mum won't let me get her a proper diamond, you know?" He chuckles, smiling to himself. "Anyway, we told her family she was pregnant afterward, but anyone who could do math would figure it out. They've had years to say something to us, but they never have. I guess because in their minds I did the right thing by marrying her, anyway."

Haggis raises his leg against a tree, and my dad braces my shoulder. "The point of this whole story is that it's normal for relationships to have problems. Your mum and I were twenty-two and suddenly expectin' a baby. We relied on her family a lot, too. So, it was awkward, knowing that we went against our religion and how they must've felt without telling us. They kept things deep inside, and we knew that. We argued a lot about it. One night . . ." He pauses and clears his throat. "It got so bad that I suggested I just move back to Scotland."

"But you didn't," I murmur, unable to think about what would've happened if he did.

"No." Dad sighs. "I didn't. Thankfully." His eyes meet mine. "Listen, the point I am trying to make is, no relationship is always easy. Even the best ones have had to endure. Even the ones that seem rock solid have had moments where it seemed like there was no path forward. Maybe you and Daisy aren't meant to be together. That's a real possibility. But I don't think this fight gets to be the reason. Does this, what's happened between you, get to make that decision? Or can you both make it back to where you were before this whole internet thing started?"

I turn my gaze to the bare trees stretching their limbs above us, as if they want to get tangled with the skyscrapers. "I'll try."

"Good." Dad kisses the top of my head, his beard tickling the side of my face. "That's all your mum and I ask."

CHAPTER THIRTY-THREE
DAISY

I notice Noah gazing at me across the room all through orchestra. As Ms. Silverstein dismisses us and I pack up my violin, I can't shake the sight of his blue eyes—or stop wondering why he's looking at me in the first place. We haven't spoken to each other since that awkward conversation outside Amal's apartment.

That doesn't mean I haven't wanted to reach out and touch him every single day I pass by his chair to go into the storage room.

But I don't. Instead, I wait until everyone else has packed away their instruments and left the room before heading inside myself.

I nearly jump out of my skin when I feel a hand on my left arm after I slide my violin case into its cubby.

I whirl around, thinking—maybe praying—for a split

second that it's Noah and we're finally going to talk. My heart plummets when I realize it's not him.

It's Beaux.

His cold, clammy hand is touching the sleeve of my pale blue sweater, his fingers hovering near the edge of its three-quarter sleeves.

"Don't touch me." The words come out softly, but I step back into the wall, rustling the violins and violas nestled in their cubbies.

"I knew if I just said hi then you would've ignored me, Differently Abled," Beaux simpers. "Your left hand was all bunched up during practice." It still is now. "Are you okay?"

"I'm fine." A lie, but I don't need to tell Beaux anything.

"Well, I was just trying to help," he continues, his finger sliding down into the crook of my elbow. "How do you get your hand unstuck anyway?"

I open my mouth, willing the words to make their way up my throat faster. "Look, I don't—I don't need your help, okay? With anything. Leave me alone."

"Fine." Beaux tuts as he drops his hand away from me. "Be that way."

•   •   •

I am about to turn in the direction of the subway station after school when I see the last person I expect.

"Ma?" I blink at her, as if trying to ensure that she's actually standing in front of me, wearing a coat the same shade of pink as Peruvian lilies. "What are you doing here?"

"I texted you." Ma kisses my cheek, smoothing back a stray strand of hair.

"We have to keep our phones on silent during school," I explain. "What's up?"

"Your uncle Celestino called," Ma tells me. "The food pantry at St. Peregrine's is understaffed today, and he was wondering if we could help out. I decided to just come and pick you up."

"Sure." I smile. "That sounds nice." It'll give me something else to think about besides the feeling of Beaux's hand on my left arm. I get to spend time with my mom, outside our apartment and the flower shop, too.

After taking the train from the Times Square subway station, we arrive at St. Peregrine's. Its light brown exterior is already more welcoming than St. Vincent de Paul's steely gray, and that's even before Father Holt greets us when we step inside.

Uncle Celestino, a towering man with a chestnut-brown goatee, hugs Ma and me. "Glad you could make it," he says. "Why don't I take you into the fellowship hall? You can check that all the bags have the right amount of groceries."

"Wherever you need us." Ma unbuttons her coat. "Is Grace here?"

"Not today." My uncle's eyes get misty. "She's rehearsing for the play her school's putting on in May. She's one of the leads," he adds, grinning. He's mostly raised my cousin on his own and is always endlessly proud of her accomplishments in theater. She's only twelve, but it won't be long until she's on Broadway. I bet Uncle Celestino will be front row at her school play. He wouldn't miss it for the world

"Tell her we said good luck." Ma folds her coat over her arm. "Let us know when ticket sales are."

"I will." Uncle Celestino opens the doors to the fellowship hall, gesturing to the closest table and disappearing without saying anything else.

But as we sit down, closer to each other than we've been in who knows how long, I try to push down the pit that has taken root in my stomach. *Why even ask about ticket sales?* I grouse. *You won't show up. Or if you do, you won't stay long enough to congratulate her. Grace will sing her heart out, but it's not like you'll—*

"Daisy." Ma's voice jerks me out of my petty tirade. "Did you hear me?"

"No." My cheeks burn as I unbutton my own coat and lay it over the back of the chair. "What'd you say? Sorry."

"Are you okay?"

Those three words hang in the small space between us and carry so much more weight than they should because we barely talk as it is—much less about me breaking up with Noah.

Ma squeezes my left hand, her slightly wizened fingers tight around my knuckles. "You don't need to lie," she murmurs. "Not to me. Io sono tua madre."

That makes me smile the tiniest bit, how her voice lilts differently in Italian. It feels awkward for her to be checking in on me this way. But she's trying, so I can try, too.

"Then no." I sigh, pulling a blue tote bag toward me and checking the amount of instant mashed potatoes inside. "Not really."

Ma rustles through her own blue tote bag, dragging her finger down a list. "You haven't said anything other than you broke up with him." Her brown eyes—mine exactly—soften when she looks at me. "Would you like to talk about why?"

"Not really," I admit. Ma turns in her chair, folding her hands on her belly, waiting for me to continue.

"Ma, you were there. You heard what he said." My voice is as hoarse as my strings being played by an untreated bow at the end. "He said he doesn't see me as disabled."

"You broke up with him because he said he didn't see you as disabled," Ma repeats back at me. I nod. "Daisy." She pauses, her hand around mine again. "Did you explain to him why what he said was wrong?"

"I . . ." My voice trails off. "I think I tried to?"

Ma's brow furrows. "What did you say exactly?"

Tears itch at my eyes, wanting to come out and flow down my cheeks. So, I'm grateful for the muscle spasm that makes my fingernails dig into my palm; it keeps me from crying. "I said he didn't see me as a full person. That he's not seeing my disability."

Ma squeezes my hand. "It's not a bad word," I remind her.

"Did Noah ever say it was?"

I whisper, "No," but it comes out more as a sob.

"Then maybe he just doesn't understand." Ma rubs circles on my back.

"It's not my job to teach him," I mumble, wiping at my face.

"I know that." She's quiet for a moment. "Have you talked to Noah since?"

I shake my head. "Not really."

"Do you want to?" she asks. "Explain why you're so angry?"

I don't tell her how he watched me today, or how much I wanted to just hold his hand. Or even what happened with Beaux, because right now, only one member of the orchestra is on my mind. So instead I just say, "Yes."

Noah (9:17 p.m.): Daisy? Can we talk?

5,739 likes

e7string Check out these stills from their episode of The Hope Baker Hour! Do you think Noah's hamming up how in love he is with Daisy for the cameras? #naisy

BassLadyDaphne He sees past her disability! How amazing! #naisy

BeauxLikeBow Allow me to barf into this metaphorical paper bag. #naisy

e7string I heard he came to his senses and dumped her.

CHAPTER THIRTY-FOUR
DAISY

It's the Friday before Valentine's Day, the day our episode of *The Hope Baker Hour* airs. Since the show airs in the morning, by the time I walk into the orchestra room after lunch, everyone knows about it.

The murmurs start as soon as I walk in and cross the floor to get into the storage room and retrieve my violin.

"Did you see Facebook?"

"How about Instagram?"

"On YouTube . . ."

"There's a new BuzzFeed article . . ."

"I can't believe . . ."

Each syllable, each word, is like a snake crawling up my arm, injecting venom into my bloodstream until all I feel is numbness coating my skin.

I can't even look at Noah, who I walk past while both entering and exiting the storage room.

No matter how much I want to talk to him.

Especially since he texted me last night.

Ms. Silverstein calls our class to order and leads us through options for the spring concert in May. All fast, bouncy pieces. The embodiment of green leaves and the flourishing butterfly garden at the Bronx Zoo.

I'm not sure if I pay attention to most of the class, feeling both the empty chair next to me where Mazhar would sit and the distance between me and Noah like a black hole that's expanding to swallow everything around it.

A few bassists smile at me; a violist tells me I did great. I swallow all their praise like it's honey-flavored cough syrup, if only because I don't have the energy to do anything else. I think Ms. Silverstein gives me a concerned look, but I push my way out of the orchestra room once the bell rings. Only when I'm in the hallway, away from the rest of the senior class orchestra, do I begin to calm down.

Slightly.

But then I feel someone tug me backward by my violin case, and I realize that I never put my instrument back in the storage room.

I assume it's Noah, and I turn around, unsure of what to say.

But the eyes mine settle on are green. Not blue.

They're Beaux Beckworth's.

"What the—" I yank the strap of my violin case, wincing as it hits my shoulder. "What was that for? How many times do I have to tell you not to touch me?"

"I just want to talk," he says, innocent.

"We have five minutes to get to our next class," I tell him as if he doesn't already know this information. "Make it quick."

Beaux's eyes flash. "Do you think you're special, Differently Abled?"

I scrunch up my face. "Why are you—"

"Oh, c'mon." Beaux takes a step toward me, and I take a step back, trying to remember the self-defense techniques I was taught in PE last year, just in case. "You got on TV. Everyone saw you. People love you. So, I just want to know how you *feel* about all of this."

My tongue sticks to the roof of my mouth. ". . . I . . . I don't feel special or anything."

"But why?" Beaux prods, malice seeping into his voice. "Everyone *thinks* you are. You know, I used to think it might be hard for you, being retarded and all. Then I thought, it was lucky you found Noah to love you. But it turns out it's not, and it's not just Noah. Everyone at this academy gives you special treatment, and Juilliard, too." My stomach drops out from under me, as if a trapdoor opened beneath it. He made that Instagram post.

"You're e7string. You're the one that made that post calling me a . . ." I can't bring myself to say the word. I won't give Beaux that satisfaction.

"Seriously?" Beaux clenches his teeth, and the words barely come out. He takes another step toward me. "You can't say it?" He waits a beat. "Why?"

"Because." The word dissipates in my mouth. "Because it—it doesn't . . ."

"Matter?" Beaux spits. "Daisy, it means everything."

"No." I close my eyes, shaking my head. "No, it doesn't."

"You're not listening to me," he seethes. "The only reason you got into this academy is because of your disability. You don't actually *belong* here. You know that. Now the rest of the world does, too." *No*, I desperately want to tell him. *You're wrong.*

Beaux grabs my left arm again, gazing down at it, fascinated. His fingers tighten around my perpetually bent wrist.

"I've told you!" The words burst out of me as I take another step away from him, trying to wrench my hand from his grip. His eyes gleam. "Don't touch—"

I gather my strength to pull my arm out of Beaux's tight grip, but he lets go of me. That's when I fall backward down the stairs, hitting my head on my violin case as I tumble to the bottom, my screams caught somewhere in my throat.

CHAPTER THIRTY-FIVE
DAISY

When the young doctor walks in, I immediately count my blessings that I sent my parents to the waiting room. I don't want to talk to him in front of them, their sad eyes watching me explain what happened.

"Hi," he says. "I'm Dr. Mohrweis, and I'll be taking care of you today. Can you tell me why you're here? What happened?"

I explain everything. Beaux coming up to me after orchestra. How he taunted me and grabbed my arm.

"That's when I fell down the stairs," I finish, staring at my hands in my lap, then up at the doctor.

"Can I take a listen to you?" he asks kindly.

"Sure." I sit up straighter. He presses the cold dime of his stethoscope to my chest, the quiet in this small room making my heart pound in my ears. He moves around to my back and instructs me to breathe.

He performs a cranial nerve exam, having me move my eyes, follow his finger, stick out my tongue, raise my eyebrows, smile, and turn my head from side to side against his hand, watching each piece intently.

"Everything looks good," Dr. Mohrweis declares. "But since you fell from a high height, it's best we keep you here for observation. Just for a few hours," he adds at my panicked face. "All to make sure you're okay. You can have visitors if you want."

"I don't want my parents back here," I blurt out. Am I surprised Ma closed the flower shop and Dad managed to get away from work to take care of me? Yes. But do I need the wrath and worry only Italian parents are capable of? No. It's too overwhelming right now.

"Okay, we will say that you are resting," Dr. Mohrweis says. "I'll go out into the waiting room and talk to them for a bit. I'll be back to check on you soon, okay?"

He leaves the room, and I let myself lie back on the pillows. The fluorescent lights are so bright they burn my eyes, making my sore body hurt even more.

I've been disabled my entire life. I've clawed my way up to orchestral excellence. I'm really good at what I do. But no one has ever wanted to hurt me because of those things.

I don't even realize that I'm crying until the doctor returns to my room. "Daisy?" he asks, walking to my bedside immediately. "Are you in any pain?"

"No." I sniff, wiping my eyes with my sleeve. He presents

me with a tissue box. "I—I *always* have to try harder than any-one else in my life, especially at school, and I—" Taking a tissue, I cram it to my eyes until I can feel the pressure. "Sorry."

"You have nothing to apologize for, Daisy," Dr. Mohrweis assures me in a low voice. "I came in here because there's some-one else in the waiting room who asked to see you. A boy? He said his name was Noah." I sit up straight too fast, letting him guide me back down with practiced hands as my body screams at me. "He says he has your violin. Do you want to see him?"

I should say no. I should just stew in this bed until the doctor tells me I can leave. Instead, I say yes.

The doctor returns with Noah in the doorway, who waits for him to walk away before running the rest of the way into my room. He opens his arms, and I collapse into sobs against his shoulder. Not out of relief that he's here, but because I need to cry to someone. I can't figure out how to talk to him anymore, no matter how much I want to. But right now, I just need him, no matter how complicated it makes things between us.

"Daisy!" Noah gasps in my ear. He's crying, too. "Thank God you're okay. Thank God."

"Why are you here?" I let go of him, and he sits in a chair next to the bed, cradling my violin case to his chest with one hand while wiping his eyes with the other.

My case looks weird in his long arms, like it's entirely too small.

"I had to make sure you were okay," he murmurs. "I—I've

wanted to talk to you." My heart leaps into my throat. "But I—I know things between us aren't . . ." He shakes his head. "The whole academy's talking about what happened. There are rumors Beaux will be expelled. I wanted to bring you your violin, too. Before anyone could get to it."

"Thank you." I try to swallow, but it gets stuck. Taking the case from him, I lay it across my lap. "One of the clasps is broken," I murmur, my fingers lingering on the tarnished metal. "But that's okay. I can fix—"

My words are cut off when I open the case. It's the same case I've had since I got accepted into the academy. I know its crushed red velvet interior, its rosin pocket, how snugly my bow fits inside. And I know my violin inside better than anything else in the world.

Or rather, I did.

My violin lies in pieces. Its neck snapped as easily as if it were a twig, the strings splayed around it like fallen leaves, the bridge split in two. Its body cracked completely in half.

Exactly how my heart feels.

"Wh-why did this happen?" I whisper, not looking at Noah, not wanting to look anywhere but the shattered pieces of my instrument. "What did I do to deserve this?"

"Daisy." Noah whispers my name. If this happened a month ago, I would let myself curl into its cadence. Now I don't even move.

"It's okay," he continues, the words rushing out of his mouth.

"I—I'll buy you a new violin." I snap my gaze to his, wincing at the soreness.

"No," I spit, my arms curling around my case protectively. "Not this again. You can't just throw money at me because your family has it and mine doesn't. I don't need your charity."

"I'm not throwing—" Noah clears his throat, his voice soft. "Daisy, this is different than some random check. Our Juilliard auditions are in less than a month. You can't exactly audition without your instrument."

"I know that," I whisper, feeling like every word I speak will reduce me to pieces like the instrument in my lap. "But I—I'm not taking your money. I'm not using the money *The Hope Baker Hour* gave us, either."

"Why are you being so stubborn about this?" Noah says, his voice breaking. "You need—"

"Don't tell me what I need!" I sob, my body screaming at me again as tears stream down my cheeks, landing on the wood and steel in my lap. "I know what I need. I need a new violin!"

"Then why can't I help you get that?" Noah whispers. "Daisy, please."

"I don't need your money. Or you. Get out." I bury my face in my hands, listening as Noah stands up from the chair and walks away.

I don't want to look at him, or what remains of my violin.

CHAPTER THIRTY-SIX

NOAH

"A peanut butter bacon burger?" Douglas glances from our tray of food in his hands to my face. "This is why you pulled me away from date night?"

After leaving the hospital, I took a Lyft to his apartment. He and Levi were dressed in pressed slacks, silk shirts, and, in my brother's case, smelled like pepper and oranges from his cologne. I felt guilty for not texting first. But I knew if anyone would understand how important a violin is, it's Douglas.

He agreed to get dinner with me instead. I slide into our wooden booth, uncapping my cup of peanut butter sauce. "Not exactly." Douglas sips from his ale, the foam coating the top of his lip, waiting for me to elaborate. "I need help." My lower lip trembles.

He raises his eyebrows above his horn-rimmed glasses. "What's wrong?"

I pour the peanut butter sauce on top of the bacon, and crunch into my burger, hoping that the combination of sweet and salty will calm my nerves.

Tears slide down my cheeks and into my food.

"Noah." Douglas reaches across the table, taking both of my wrists in his hands, his own burger and cheese fries forgotten between us. "Talk to me."

I take my glasses off, holding them between my fingers as I look up at the ceiling. The lights turn into muddled blobs across my vision as I tell Douglas how Daisy fell down the stairs, how her violin broke, and how she doesn't want me—or anyone—to get her a new instrument.

"Our auditions are soon," I finish, dragging my arm across my face. "If Daisy doesn't have a violin—"

"Then she can't audition," my brother finishes. "You think she doesn't know that?"

"Well, of course she knows." My hand's crammed into my hair, probably smearing stray bits of peanut butter sauce through the strands. "But—"

"You can't fix Daisy's problems," Douglas interjects. He gently takes my hand from my hair and my glasses from my fingers, polishing them on the sleeve of his maroon shirt. "No matter how much you care about her, okay? Maybe she feels like she has to handle this on her own. You need to respect that."

Respect. Like how she told me I didn't respect her the day of our *Hope Baker Hour* taping.

I nod, sliding my glasses back on after he hands them to me.

"Look." Douglas takes another sip of ale and eats a forkful of cheese fries. "I'm not going to pretend I know what it's like for Daisy right now. Even the Moray Stage's comments section is exploding about you two. Everyone wants you guys on to do a collab video. But let me ask you a question." He waves his hand, his platinum wedding ring winking in the lights. "Do you understand *why* she won't let anyone give her money for a new violin?"

"She said she doesn't need charity," I explain around my mouthful of peanut butter and bacon.

A knowing smile unfurls across my brother's face. "What if it's not charity?"

I blink at him. "What are you talking about?"

"Give me a few days." Douglas gets to his feet, drawing his broad body up to his full height. "As for how you are going to get her back?" My mouth drops open, but he continues. "That part is entirely up to you." He motions for me to stand and when I do, he loops his arm around my back, hugging me. "Now, let's get you home. I ditched my husband for you, so I have some making up to do."

• • •

That night, while my parents are busy performing with their orchestra, I sit in the living room with a cup of tea.

The familiar motions—the kettle boiling, letting the tea steep, adding honey and milk—calm me as much as Haggis curling up in my lap.

I scroll through Instagram, with only the soundtrack of the

Upper East Side below me. Taxicabs. Car horns. Trains rattling across tracks. Nothing out of the ordinary, nothing to suggest the chaos swirling around in my own head.

In Mazhar and Amal's pictures of San Francisco—from Ghirardelli Square to the Golden Gate Bridge to their college campuses—they both have huge grins on their faces, their arms wrapped around each other.

After I like a picture of them eating ice cream to celebrate Mazhar's live audition, I click over to my explore page and notice something else: the interview Daisy and I did for *The Hope Baker Hour.*

The still—Daisy and me sitting on that silver couch, coordinated in navy blue—makes my stomach lurch and my dinner threaten to come back up. But I tap it anyway, my tea turning sour in my mouth as it plays.

Watching the interview for the first time, I notice how uncomfortable Daisy is. She's fidgeting, just like she was that day in Principal Loman's office. Hope Baker is completely oblivious. Actually, so am I. I'm carrying myself as if that soundstage were in Carnegie Hall, trying to be as poised as possible. I don't even look at Daisy when I tell the entirety of New York City that I don't see her as disabled. I'm so disgustingly certain that I'm doing the right thing.

That's why she walked off the set. That's why she broke up with me. That's why she wouldn't accept the check, why she won't let me give her money for a new violin.

I was ableist.

To the girl I'm most definitely in love with.

I place my mug on the coffee table in front of me, my phone alongside it, before slumping back on the couch, closing my eyes.

All I care about right now is apologizing to her.

And I have no idea how to do that.

CHAPTER THIRTY-SEVEN
DAISY

Noah is standing at the entrance of St. Vincent de Paul, wearing a white dress shirt and a kilt.

"Hi," I say, ignoring how much I want to reach out and touch him. "What are you doing here?"

"Hi." The word almost lost in his mouth, his voice as breathy as mine. "Um. Is it okay if I sit with you?"

"Sure, Noah," Dad says quickly, before I can open my mouth again.

"Welcome to St. Vincent de Paul," Ma adds.

Both of them are entirely too calm about the fact that Noah has showed up at our church, but then I realize that they're keeping up appearances. The Abanos try never to make a fuss, but especially not in church.

"Thank you."

When we walk inside, Mrs. Pecora presses the program into

my hands, explaining: "Today's sermon is about God's love! Isn't that wonderful, Daisy?"

"Yes," I say automatically, both a church lady's favorite response to almost everything and the quickest way to get away from her.

"What a joyous morning," she adds happily, her voice honey sweet. "Dear, sit up front. Father Benedetti reserved that pew for you and your family."

I blink, but simply say thank you, and dip my fingers in the holy water font.

In the sanctuary, people whisper as we walk down the aisle. Usually, the gossip is about someone eloping (Emilio Abate supposedly married Flora Bellini in Vegas last week) or pregnancy (Gianna Cipriani, who brings raspberry streusel to fellowship, who already has a son in the youth group, and who's been married to her husband for over ten years, but whatever floats your boat, parishioners).

We walk to the front of the church past our usual pew in the very back, and I notice people's eyes on us. They're whispering about me and Noah, and suddenly I know exactly why. Everyone in this church either saw or heard about our appearance on *The Hope Baker Hour.* And now that we're here *together?* Good Lord.

They probably think that Noah is an angel for being selfless enough to love me, too. They view me as some sort of divine blessing, despite the fact that this morning was the first time all weekend I bothered to shower, put on actual clothes, and have Ma braid my hair.

No one knows about my fall down the stairs.

By the time we're seated in front of the altar, before a complex stained-glass window that washes colors across the large wooden crucifix overlooking the congregation, my left hand is curled into a fist at my side, and I have to forcibly pry it open with my right to grab the worn hymnal in front of me.

Noah slides into the pew next to me. His eyes flit to mine, and my stomach swooshes when he gestures to the book in my hands with his own. "Is there a page we open to?"

I tell him the number, and soon the blue-robed choir leads us in "I Have Loved You." Noah's baritone melds with my soprano in a way that makes me ache. I never realized our singing voices went so well together, too.

Afterward, Father Benedetti faces us, beaming. "Peace be with you!" he says as we echo back, "And with your spirit."

"Today," the priest continues grandly, "we are here to discuss God's love. Ruminate on it, contemplate what His love means and how you, as His disciples, can reflect that back into the world that He, Himself, created."

Father Benedetti waits a few beats, letting his opening notes sink in. "Now, I know," he says, "that social media is often not the best tool for such a momentous, important task. However, this past week, because of one of our own, we've been reminded of the power of God's love."

My left arm locks up in a muscle spasm at his words. I know where this is going, even before his eyes meet mine. I should have figured it out when Mrs. Pecora directed us to the front pew.

Father Benedetti has crafted an entire sermon around *me*.

"For those of you who don't know, Daisy Abano, a devout follower of Christ, has made the world aware of her talents as a violinist," Father Benedetti explains. "From YouTube to television. All the while pushing past the tumultuous circumstances of her condition."

Blood starts to simmer in my veins, but I stay in the pew, no matter how much I want to walk out of the church. Ma puts her hand on my arm. If this were a normal service, I'd lean into her touch, but right now, it just makes my skin crawl. She shouldn't have to placate me about the words our priest is saying. But she is.

Noah remains stiff beside me.

"We all know," Father Benedetti continues, "that God hasn't given Daisy's family more than they can handle. Was it His choice to give Daisy a condition in order to bless her family, as with each hardship comes a lesson He desires to teach them? Perhaps. However." He pauses, long enough for nausea to grip my stomach. "We also know that *prayer* is a miracle in itself. Communicating our hopes with God in order to manifest them into the world is what we do as Catholics. And I believe that if we, as a congregation, *prayed* for God to release Daisy from the burden of her condition, that He would hear us."

"Amen!" someone agrees, sending a ripple across the church.

I put my hand over my mouth, whispering "This isn't happening" against my fingers.

"Now!" Father Benedetti commands. "Let us—"

"You should be ashamed of yourself!"

I take my hand away from my mouth, staring at the Bible and hymnal in front of me, frozen, terrified that I actually spoke out against my priest in front of everyone.

But I didn't say anything.

The voice was low and deep.

"Sorry?" The coldness of his voice quiets the entire church. "Do you have a reason for your rudeness, my son?"

"As a matter of fact, I do." The congregation turns toward the speaker, and my stomach drops down to my ankles. It's Noah, standing up next to me, glaring at my priest.

"And what would that be?" Father Benedetti asks.

"Because you're disrespecting Daisy," Noah replies. "She's a member of your church, isn't she? You had this whole church pray for her when she was born, didn't you?"

He remembers I told him that?

"I did," Father Benedetti says. "As a priest, I pray for everyone who may need it. Daisy was in dire straits when she was born. Prayer was a great comfort to her family—"

"So why are you weaponizing that comfort now?" Noah retorts, walking up to the altar, his kilt brushing against his knees.

"On the contrary, I'm calling upon God to heal Daisy of her condition," Father Benedetti explains with an air of superiority. "It's a burden that none of us can imagine, but that He can *erase* for her. Surely, a young man like yourself can understand that at least."

I rise to my feet, sidestepping out of the pew and walking over to them as if I'm just receiving communion.

"If you were truly a man of God," I say, positioning myself between Noah and Father Benedetti, "then you'd understand that He doesn't make mistakes."

Father Benedetti turns purple. "How dare you insult me and the Lord in His own house!" he shouts. Behind me, Noah takes my hand in his own, as naturally as holding his bow frog, which makes my heart crack open. "This church has been nothing but accepting of you ever since we learned about your condition, and this is how you—"

"*Stop!*" My voice cracks against the stone walls and stained-glass windows. "Stop saying 'condition'! It's a disability. I have a *disability!*"

"Fine." Father Benedetti clucks his tongue, a sound that somehow echoes throughout the sanctuary. "It's still something that God can heal you of if we pray—"

"No." I square my shoulders, squeezing Noah's hand. He squeezes mine back. "I'm leaving." I spin around on my heel, and Noah and I start walking up the aisle, the murmurs of the church filling my ears.

I glance at my parents, expecting them to be furious with us for making a scene. But I find something more complicated in their eyes. Dad looks confused. Ma is mad—her shoulders reach up to her ears—but she also has tears in her eyes. Dad goes to stand up, but she puts her hand on his shoulder and says, "Let them go," not unkindly, her shoulders relaxing. Halfway up, Father Benedetti's words stop us. "Daisy," he implores, making my left foot snag on the floor. Noah braces me so I don't fall, the hand not holding mine lingering on my shoulder. "Have you even given *thought* about what prayer could do for your condition? Have you discussed it with God?"

I turn to him, making the sign of the cross and ignoring the colorful light popping across my vision from the stained-glass windows. "I don't have to talk to God about my cerebral palsy. But right now, He's telling me to get the *hell* away from you."

Then, together, Noah and I run the rest of the way out of St. Vincent de Paul, not stopping until we reach the bottom of the stairs.

CHAPTER THIRTY-EIGHT
DAISY

We're both out of breath once we spill onto the street, but that doesn't stop me from rounding on Noah anyway.

"What," I wheeze, "are you doing here?"

Noah hesitates. Now that we're out of the church, away from Father Benedetti and the prying eyes of the congregation, we've both lost our bravado. Noah crams his hand into his hair; his eyes drift down to his shoes. "Daisy, I had to talk to you somehow."

"Why did you come here?" I repeat, gesturing to the hulking church behind us.

"Do you really come to this place every week?" Noah asks. "To have people pray away your disability?"

"Oh." I scoff, narrowing my eyes. "So, you've remembered I'm disabled now, huh?"

"What are you—" He pinches the bridge of his nose. That reddish line from his glasses is still there. His hair is more rumpled than usual, too, the bags beneath his eyes a deeper purple. "Would you rather I just let you walk away from me on television sets and in your church?"

"Of course not!" My throat tugs. "But, Noah! You're almost as bad as they are!" Salt starts to sting my eyes, and I try to wipe my tears away with the heels of my hands as I sniff. *"You're doing the same thing."*

"No." Noah shakes his head, his eyes wide. "Daisy, I'm not."

"Yes!" Tears roll down my cheeks, but this time, I don't bother stopping them. "You're just like my church, wanting to look *beyond my burden.*"

Noah steps backward, his shoulders crumpling in on themselves. "That's what you think I meant?" he whispers.

"How else *could* you mean it?" I fire back. "Noah, look, the reason I didn't speak to you before I fell down the stairs is because I—" My lower lip trembles. "I don't *want* to lose you, okay? But what am I supposed to do with someone who doesn't see me for all that I am? You were *ableist.*" I almost choke on the word. It settles like a weight on my chest. "To me. Do you even realize how painful that moment was? Being rejected like that by someone I *care* about so much?"

"Daisy." Tears spring to his eyes now, too. "Can I—can I say something, please?"

I don't want to leave him, so I nod.

"I watched the interview." Noah presses his hands to his chest. My eyes grow wide. I haven't watched it yet, and I wasn't going to. I lived it. I don't need to be on Hope Baker's stage ever again. "I heard what I said, and I am *so sorry.*

"I tried to stand up for you, without thinking." He swallows. "I *never* meant to hurt you. But I did, and I *promise* to keep learning from my mistakes. Because"—Noah takes a breath of his own, vibrato shivering through his ribs as he exhales a foggy cloud—"I am in love with you, Daisy Abano."

I stare at him, my hands over my mouth. The fingers on my left dig into the knuckles on my right, but I don't care. I barely feel them.

"You don't have to say anything," Noah sputters, his voice high. "But I had to come here and tell you that. I love you, Daisy."

The skirt of my dress brushes against Noah's kilt as I take a step toward him, tilting my face up to meet his. Standing up on my tiptoes, I wrap my arms around his shoulders as he tentatively places his hands on my waist.

Our noses brush together, his glasses sliding down the tiniest bit.

"I love you, too, Noah," I whisper before pressing my lips to his.

Our kisses are warm and frantic despite the New York winter around us. Noah cups my cheeks in his hands as he kisses me back, the pressure of his fingertips making me dizzy in the best kind of way.

Our hearts thrum in time with each other as I open my eyes, not wanting to look away from him.

CHAPTER THIRTY-NINE
DAISY

Ma texts me right as Mass is over. Normally, she'd be at fellowship, but I guess me standing up to Father Benedetti and storming out with my boyfriend is bigger than Mrs. Cipriani's raspberry streusel.

Ma (11:02 a.m.): Go to the flower shop.

Noah and I went to Grand Ferry Park, to make up for lost weeks not kissing, but after both of us read Ma's message, he kisses my forehead. His lips linger there for longer than usual as we listen to the sounds of the water and the city.

"I'll go with you."

"It's better if I do this alone."

We compromise, and he rides the subway with me to Rockefeller Center. But before I go inside Ottavia's Flower

Arrangements (which has a WE'RE CLOSED sign hanging on the door), he kisses me again.

"I'll see you at school," he murmurs, smiling.

I watch him walk away, then duck into the store, the bells overhead jingling as the door closes.

The shop is silent. Just Ma, Dad, and a selection of flowers for February: purplish-pink stargazer lilies, peach lisianthus, and, of course, deep red roses.

"Where are Nonna and Nonno?" I ask.

"Home," Dad supplies. "Holly's with them." He glances at Ma, who's glaring at me, red-faced. I shrink back, but only a little. "We wanted to talk to you al—"

"Daisy!" Ma bursts out, coming out from behind the counter. "Cursing at your priest? Running out of church with—with *Noah*?"

"You've never acted like that before at church." Dad places his hand on the small of Ma's back, turning to her. "I don't think we've ever been so disappointed."

"Disappointed?" Ma repeats, folding her arms across her chest and staring up at him. "Madon, Sal! We're mortified! How could she do something so disrespectful—"

"For God's sake, let me talk!" I yell. My parents turn in my direction, as if they forgot I was there in the first place. "Is me running out of church *really* what you're focused on right now?"

"Church is a sacred place, Daisy," Ma whispers even though

we're the only ones in the shop. "I understand you got upset, but you can't just—"

"Stand up for myself?" I splutter, glaring at her. "Ma, I saw your face when I left! You understood, at least in that moment. Or did you have a change of heart? Would you rather I *prayed* to be fixed?"

"Sweetheart." The color drains from her face until she's as white as calla lilies.

"You know we don't think that," Dad adds.

"But you're mad because I cursed at a man who does!" I throw my arms out at my sides, my left one becoming tighter the more stressed I get. "Look." Sighing, I drop my arms. "Do you know what I . . . Can I ask something?"

Both Ma and Dad shift, and the shop's wooden floor creaks underneath their shoes. Outside, a family laughs about arriving at the ice rink.

"When was the last show of mine you went to?"

"Daisy," Ma tuts, annoyed, making the fingernails on my left hand chew into my palm. "What does that have anything to do with this? We went to the winter holiday concert."

"Before that."

Neither of them says anything, the weight of calculating dates and counting backward too heavy in the air between us.

"Exactly." I wipe at my face with my coat sleeve. "It was the fall musical when I was a freshman."

"We're busy," Ma snips. "We have to keep the shop going

and a roof over our heads. Would you rather have to move in with Nonna and Nonno just so we can be at shows more?"

My mouth falls open. "No, but—"

"That was around the time we found out your mom was pregnant, too," Dad interjects, his calmer voice throwing both of us. "I remember."

"Of course she was," I whisper. We thought she just had food poisoning after fellowship one Sunday. "It makes so much sense."

"Daisy, what has gotten into you?" Ma chides. "First, you completely embarrass us in church—"

"*I* embarrassed you?" Blood starts to pound in my ears. "Were you not—"

"And now you're saying you resent Holly?" Ma fires off as if I hadn't said anything. "You don't love your own sister, is that it?"

"No!" I bury my face in my hands. "Of course I love her!"

Ma makes a noise of exasperation from somewhere in her throat. "What does she have to do with any of this?"

"Everything!" My voice hurts from how clogged my throat has become, holding back tears. "She has everything to do with this! You—you've picked her over me." A thought takes root in my chest and flies out of my mouth before I can even really make sense of it. "Is it because—because she's not disabled?!"

If my words were notes played on a violin, they would be high Es and As only, no room to be mellowed out by the lower strings. A truth so painful it can only be shouted within the confines of my family and our flowers.

"Answer me!" I yell. "You got your perfect daughter after all. Is that what this is about?"

"You're being ridiculous," Ma mutters, almost to herself, like she doesn't want any of us to hear.

Dad shakes his head. "Of course we haven't picked her over you."

Neither of them pushed back against my question. Instead, they let it take seed, burrowing down so deep that they won't need to think about it.

"You think that I'm okay now. And I get it. Holly's three, she needs her parents, but I still need you, too!" Tears are pouring in rivers down my cheeks, but I don't even bother wiping at them. "For God's sake, do you even realize how *screwed up* this is?"

"Daisy." Dad reaches for me, but I back away into the counter.

"Sweetheart." Ma clucks her tongue. "I know you've had a difficult time lately." *Is that what she calls it? I still don't have a violin, and my Juilliard audition in just weeks away.* I nearly choke out a laugh, but then her eyes harden. "But don't you dare tell us that we don't have time for you. We're working so hard so that we can provide for this whole family. We're giving you everything we can. You know that."

She turns on her heel and storms away, slamming the door to the back room before I can say anything.

All I can do is look at my dad.

"She's right." He sighs, his shoulders heavy. "I'm not sure what you want to hear right now."

"Nothing." I push off the counter and exit the shop, walking directly into Noah.

"Whoa." I peer up at him. My eyes might be red from crying, but he doesn't draw attention to it. "What are you doing here?"

"I wanted to make sure you were all right." Noah takes my left hand in his. "So, I stuck around. I didn't hear anything," he adds, holding up his phone. "I was around the corner talking to Gavin." He shakes his head, like shaking off a memory. "But anyway, tell me what happened."

"Noah." I close my eyes, feeling more tears trickle down my cheeks. "I'm not okay right now."

He nods knowingly, and then, as gently as he did all those months ago, he presses his sleeve to my cheeks, wiping away the wetness. "Then let's walk until you are."

CHAPTER FORTY
NOAH

The Monday after Mazhar and Amal return from San Francisco, the four of us end up around a table at Café Istanbul once school ends. Our heads are bent together over ramekins of fırın sütlaç.

"How are things with your parents?" Amal asks.

"Fine. Awkward. Hard. I don't know. They've eased up a bit since the meeting with Principal Loman," Daisy replies.

"Right, how did that go?" Mazhar asks.

"Well." Daisy eats a spoonful of baked rice pudding. "My and Beaux's parents were there, and so was Ms. Silverstein. They played the security camera footage, and I showed my broken violin." Her voice wobbles, and she pinches her nose, which reminds me of the shattered instrument sitting in crushed red velvet.

"So, what's going to happen to Beaux?" Amal has a spoonful of pudding poised in front of her mouth.

"He's being expelled." She smiles the tiniest bit, and every-one shares high fives around our table.

"That solves one problem." I take a sip of my orange soda, kissing the side of Daisy's head.

"But Beaux still has access to the internet." Daisy sips her own orange soda. "So even if he is expelled, he'll keep posting." She holds up her phone, opening Instagram, showing people's comments on the interview, most of which are stills of my and Daisy's faces:

7,007 likes

MaggieNotMary

Awww!!! He loves her despite her disability!

ThePianoDude

She's overcome so much! #naisy

ChauncyTheMusicPup

Chauncy's momma here! Noah's a sweetheart! Imagine loving someone so much to see past their conditions!

"Then we need to do something," Amal says, swallowing her own mouthful of fırın sütlaç. "You don't deserve to be treated like this."

"I know." Daisy puts her phone facedown on the table, clos-ing her eyes for a second. "But how am I supposed to take on a troll like Beaux? Or a multimillionaire talk show host with an empire who doesn't even know how wrong she is?"

"Not alone, that's for sure." I squeeze her hand, scrolling through my own Instagram feed. She squeezes mine back, just as I see something with the hashtag for our academy, #mamp, which I've followed for years. I realize now that keeping tabs on those things is so important to me because of my anxiety. I twist everything that happens on that stage into a competition, and now with therapy I'm trying not to. I stand up, thoughts racing through my brain. "Hang on."

"Where are you going?" Daisy asks as I head for the door.

"I'll be back in a second!" I call, the bells tinkling overhead as I exit the restaurant, stepping into Times Square, heading in the direction of where most of its screens are clustered.

"Noah!" Amal's voice is in my ear. I stop and turn to her. Daisy and Mazhar are huddled at the door, too. "What's going on?"

I gesture to the screen I saw on Instagram, by coincidence the same one Daisy and I saw ourselves on, paraded out for the whole city and then the rest of the world outside the five boroughs.

On the screen, Mr. Castillo is down on one knee in front of Ms. Silverstein, who has her hands on her cheeks, as they stand in front of the Music Box Theatre.

"I'm not one usually at a loss for words," Mr. Castillo says. "And I've tried to come up with an elaborate way of asking you to be my wife ever since the night I realized I was in love with you. I knew on our first date, here. When I was too nervous to say anything. And now, well, I still am. But all I need to say is: Rachel Talia Silverstein, will you marry me?"

"I love you!" Ms. Silverstein shrieks happily. "Yes! Miguel, of course I will!"

And because they aren't in an academy hallway, our orchestra conductor kisses the senior musical theater director, both of them beaming when they break apart.

"I knew it!" Mazhar hisses, jumping up and down on the balls of his feet.

"The whole academy did!" Daisy yells, turning to me, her hands clasped in front of her chest. "Did you see this on Instagram?" I nod. "Then why did you run all the way out here?"

"Because." I go to cram my hand in my hair but stop, dropping it at my side. "That's what we need to do."

Pink floods Daisy's cheeks. "Get engaged in Times Square?"

"No." I shake my head, my own cheeks warm. "We need to get on this screen again. Broadcast ourselves to this city, then the internet. This time, we need to make them see what we want them to see."

"Fight back," Daisy adds, "the way we got into this mess."

"Exactly. Change the narrative." Pushing my glasses up on my nose, I take my phone out from my khakis' pocket. "I need to call in an order at your mom's flower shop."

CHAPTER FORTY-ONE
NOAH

It's eerie being at school before almost everyone else.

Somehow, carrying a massive bouquet of pink gerbera daisies that even I can barely see over isn't helping.

"Are you sure this is a good idea?" Daisy asks from somewhere in front of me. I'm following the sound of her sneakers against the floor more than her voice.

"Sure?" I settle on saying. "We don't have much of a choice now, do we?"

"No," Daisy agrees, her violin case smacking her shoulder as she walks. "But it's not like we can just ask how to get up on the screens in Times Square in front of all the other teachers."

"But we don't even know if Ms. Silverstein or Mr. Castillo will be in the teachers' lounge this early," I say.

"They usually are," Daisy responds. "Our auditions are next week, so there isn't much time left to ask. If we—"

"When." I smile. "When we get accepted into Juilliard."

"Okay." The word shivers in her mouth, but I can tell she's smiling. Ms. Silverstein modified one of the school's extra violins for her to play at the audition. But what happens when we graduate? We haven't talked about that yet—and I doubt Daisy wants to think about being without her instrument now. *"When. When* we get accepted into Juilliard, we don't want the internet glomming on to that, either. We want to celebrate it on our own terms."

MAMP announces where each member of the senior class is going to college at graduation. The ceremony is livestreamed on their YouTube channel, which means the internet gets another piece of our story. Maybe we can't completely stop that from happening. But we can push back, spin it closer to the truth. Take back the narrative.

"Juilliard, eh?"

Mr. Castillo's voice nearly makes me drop the bouquet, but I catch the vase just before it slips through my fingers.

"Mr. Castillo!" Daisy and I chorus, our voices high. "Good morning!"

"Good morning," he chuckles, brushing dust off his book-patterned tie. "May I ask why you're here so early? And why you're carrying a tower of flowers down the hallway?"

"Well." I clear my throat, peering at him over the flowers. "See, we're here because we—um."

"To congratulate you and Ms. Silverstein," Daisy chimes in.

"On your engagement. We saw it on the screen in Times Square yesterday. We were bringing these to the teachers' lounge. They're from my mom's flower shop."

"Thank you so much!" Mr. Castillo beams, his cheeks flushed. "Rach—Ms. Silverstein's already there, actually. I was just walking back myself. Follow me."

Mr. Castillo leads us to the teachers' lounge, which is tucked away between the main office and guidance counselors' hub, opening the door. It's a sparse room, with white walls, windows looking out onto city streets, and a canvas painting of colorful music notes to lighten it up.

Ms. Silverstein is standing at the coffee station, wearing a bird-patterned dress, a paper cup that matches the academy's colors in her hand. She beams when she sees Mr. Castillo.

"I've found a few of your students, it seems," he says, matching her grin.

"Here an hour before classes start?" Ms. Silverstein strides over to us, the clack of her heels muffled on the carpet. "What's the occasion?"

"To congratulate us on our engagement, apparently." Mr. Castillo gestures to the bouquet in my arms. "Compliments of Daisy's mom's flower shop."

"Ottavia's Flower Arrangements," Daisy clarifies as Ms. Silverstein puts the vase down on a nearby table.

"Wow, these are so beautiful. Thank you both so much!" Ms. Silverstein glows. "You really didn't have to. Here, sit. We can chat for a bit. With both your Juilliard auditions coming up, I think we should."

"Congratulations," Mr. Castillo commends us as we all sit down in overstuffed armchairs. "I went to NYU, but Juilliard is obviously also a fantastic school."

"It's one of the best; both schools are." Ms. Silverstein looks at us as she sips her coffee. "Are your repertoires all prepared?" she asks.

"Yes," we say in unison. We've been practicing them at my apartment. Even more than when we were rehearsing our duet now that Daisy doesn't go to church with her family on Sundays. She says she wants to start attending St. Peregrine's after our auditions are over.

"You'll both do very well. But remember not to push yourselves too hard," she says, and I think I see her glance down at my fingers, which have now scabbed over. "I loved my time there. It's such an amazing opportunity, being around all that talent and knowing you're there *because* of your talent. If you need any help between now and your auditions next Wednesday, please let me know. I'm your orchestra conductor; it's what I'm here for."

"Yes," Mr. Castillo adds. "With auditions coming up for all the students here, we teachers really want to help however we can. We remember what it's like."

"Thank you." I clear my throat again, stopping myself before cramming my hand into my hair. "Actually, there is something we'd like to talk to you about."

"Which is?" Both teachers lean forward, and for a moment, it's quiet enough to hear the traffic press against the windows.

Daisy fidgets in her seat, her left hand bunching into a fist in her lap. "You know about how we went viral, right? Because of the concert?" They nod. "Well, we need to fight back against the internet," she continues. "And we think we know how we want to do that now, thanks to your engagement."

"Can you tell us how you managed to get on a screen in Times Square to propose, Mr. Castillo?" I ask.

"There's a company you can call," Mr. Castillo explains, immediately in teacher mode as if he's instructing us on the history of musical theater. "They can help you arrange everything. My abuelo worked with Times Square Broadcast Group before he retired and they handle things like this, too. But I'd imagine you'd have to be at least eighteen."

"Oh, I hadn't thought about that," I say. "I don't turn eighteen until May eighth."

"July twentieth," Daisy mumbles.

Ms. Silverstein twirls her engagement ring around on her finger, deep in thought. "Well, we can't exactly *do* any of this for you. We're only your teachers, but . . ." she says, looking over at Mr. Castillo.

"Wait." Daisy's brown eyes grow wide and she turns to me. "Maybe we are thinking too literally. This can be a big deal without actually being on a giant screen. Noah, what if we asked your brothers for help?"

My stomach drops. "Like, have them film a video of us and upload it to their YouTube channel?"

"Yeah!" Daisy nods so fast that her braid smacks her shoulder. "Think about it. Their fan base's comments have been *everywhere*, right?"

"We can use our hashtag, too," I say, grabbing her hands. "It's a cringey one, sure, but—"

"It's there," Daisy finishes.

"Keep your phones on you today, okay?" We turn toward Ms. Silverstein's voice. "On silent, per school policy, but don't put them in your lockers. Now, get ready for class," she adds briskly, her eyes bright as she shepherds us from the teachers' lounge. "I'll see both of you at orchestra practice."

• • •

It's not until after AP Global History that my phone flashes text messages up on its screen.

And they're from Douglas.

Douglas (3:34 p.m.): Rachel told me everything. I want you and Daisy to meet me at Carnegie Hall as soon as school lets out. I'll be waiting for you. Bring your instruments. Also, don't tell Daisy. But I pulled some strings for her.

Douglas (3:34 p.m.): Pun intended. 😉🎻

CHAPTER FORTY-TWO
DAISY

"You're sure your brother said for us to meet him here?" I ask.

"I'm sure." Noah swallows, his Adam's apple bobbing.

"You made it!" Douglas emerges from the venue, giving us hugs and beckoning us through the doors, his brown satchel swinging between his shoulders.

"Douglas?" I ask as we follow him across the vast black floor that makes our steps echo back. "What are we doing here?"

"Practicing," Douglas replies as if it's the most natural answer to any question he could've been asked. Which, for a violinist as decorated as he is, is kind of true. "Because if you can perform on these stages, you can perform anywhere."

"What did Ms. Silverstein tell you?" I ask as he opens the doors to Zankel Hall, its sleek white floor and rows of cushioned blue chairs spilling out in front of us.

"Rachel reached out and told me about your idea," Douglas explains. "Obviously, because she's your teacher, she can't get involved in this further. But I can." He takes his phone out from his back pocket, the familiar ping of FaceTime bouncing around the performance hall. Gavin's face fills the screen.

"You're there!" He beams at us. "Perfect."

"Tell them what we came up with," Douglas says.

"We were thinking you could perform here in the video," Gavin begins, making my and Noah's mouths fall open. "We can film it whenever and upload it the morning of your Juilliard auditions. We can have it broadcast on-screen in Times Square, too."

Noah and I stare at each other. "It's perfect," we say.

"Now." Douglas hands Noah his phone. He claps his hands, the sound reverberating through the theater. "Excuse me for a second."

He boosts himself up onstage and disappears into the wings, reemerging a moment later to stand center stage.

And cradled in his arms is a hard black violin case.

"Daisy," he says, reverent. "I have something for you."

It takes me a few beats to find my voice, like I'm staring at rests in bars of music, waiting to play a note.

"Douglas," I murmur, finally. "I— Thank you. But I cannot accept a gift like this."

"This isn't from me." Douglas hands the case to me,

jumping into the house and telling me to lay the case down.

"Then who?" I raise an eyebrow, placing the case on the stage's waxed floor.

"The entire *Phantom of the Opera* orchestra." Douglas beams at me as I whirl around to stare at him openmouthed again. Gavin grins from the palm of his hand. "After Noah told me what happened"—I glance at Noah, who looks down at his shoes for a brief second—"I talked to them and explained that you have a Juilliard audition the same day as Noah, and about what happened. None of us were about to let a violinist as excellent as you are walk through its doors without your instrument. We are a professional orchestra. We have connections and were able to get this for you today. I promise we didn't spend any money. Only favors!"

"Oh my God," I whisper, my left hand curling into a fist against the case. "Thank you so much, Douglas."

"Don't thank me yet." Douglas waves his hand. "Open it."

With trembling fingers, I flip up the gleaming silver clasps, gazing down at the most beautiful violin I've ever laid eyes on. A glossy brown body, with shiny metal strings stretching from the fine tuners to the scroll, lying in a cushion of blue velvet, waiting for me to play it.

And a chin rest already positioned on the right side.

"Are the strings . . . ?" I stare up at Douglas, who nods.

"They're in reverse, exactly as you play. I took the liberty of making sure of that." He smiles at me, and I let out a slow breath, taking Noah's hand in mine as he gazes down at my new violin, given to me by musicians who I can—and will—someday play beside.

"Now," Gavin says, gesturing at us through Douglas's phone screen, "get onstage."

CHAPTER FORTY-THREE
NOAH

Douglas takes a seat in the front row, propping his hand up on the armrest so Gavin can see, too.

"Who's going first?" Daisy asks once we pull up chairs and music stands, unpacking our instruments.

"Oh, you both are," Douglas says from his seat. "You can't perform your audition repertoires for the video. It'll need to be something quick, but something you've already performed. Rachel suggested your duet from the winter holiday concert."

"Something the internet already knows," Daisy murmurs, both of us sharing a glance. The stage lights flash across my glasses, and I can see them reflecting in her eyes.

"I reprinted the sheet music before I came over here." Douglas opens his satchel, removing two copies of it and handing it to us.

"Run through your scales," Gavin instructs from his phone.

"Keep your spines straight. Flush against the seat, Noah. Like Daisy."

A rush of blood fills my cheeks. "My back is straight, Gavin."

"I know bad posture when I see it," Gavin replies airily as I scoot against the chair, realizing my shoulders actually were sort of slouched. "Scales are the first thing every musician learns. Go on."

Daisy and I each run through our scales, then Douglas invites us to perform the duet. The duet he and Gavin composed, that is also everywhere online now. From Facebook to Twitter to Instagram to BuzzFeed, everyone knows this song.

They also think that they know me and Daisy, too.

Suddenly, I can't move.

After fourteen years as a cellist, scales are muscle memory. I perform every single day, whether at the academy or in my bedroom when I should be sleeping. But I am getting better at that.

Dr. Singh is proud of me.

My family is proud of me.

My friends are proud of me.

My girlfriend is proud of me.

So why am I dropping my bow?

Why are the stage lights filling my vision, pressing on my eyeballs?

Why is my breath coming from my chest in short bursts that scrabble at the walls of my throat?

Why is my heart no longer in my ribs, but in my ears?

"Noah? Can you hear me?"

Daisy's voice brings Zankel Hall slowly back into focus. Its polished wooden walls, its rows of cushioned seats, its staircases leading to the back of the theater on either side.

"I—I'm sorry," I whisper. "This"—I pick up my bow, waving it around—"it's not about me. It's about you. I shouldn't be—Daisy, if we can't pull this off, I . . ."

She rests her left hand on my cheek. Her bow, sticky from the rosin, presses against my face. "I love you," she whispers, her words making me hold my own bow to her cheek. "And your anxiety, Noah, that's as much a part of you as my cerebral palsy is of me. We don't need to apologize for ourselves. Especially not to each other."

"I love you, too." Leaning across our chairs, I kiss her onstage for a second time. And as I bring her closer to me, both of us still clutching our instruments, I'm pretty sure that the warmth between us isn't just because of the stage lights.

Daisy (5:05 p.m.): The plan is to film a video at Carnegie Hall.

Noah (5:05 p.m.): And upload it to my brothers' YouTube channel and stream in Times Square.

Mazhar (5:06 p.m.): I love this idea.

Amal (5:07 p.m.): When is all this going down?

Noah (5:08 p.m.): Douglas says we need to be at Carnegie Hall at 8 a.m. on March 3. The video will go up at 10 a.m.

Amal (5:08 p.m.): We'll be in the audience.

Mazhar (5:08 p.m.): Absolutely. We're not letting you perform to an empty house even though the whole world is gonna be watching.

CHAPTER FORTY-FOUR
NOAH

"I don't usually see you on Mondays, nor especially this late in the evening," Dr. Singh begins once I am settled in his office. Well, *settled* might be a strong word. I'm sitting on the couch, leaning forward, my legs jiggling. But at least I'm not pacing. It's almost six.

"I know."

Tonight, the sky behind Dr. Singh is streaked with deep purples and pinks, bright yellows, and fierce oranges. Manhattan at dusk.

"Do you want to talk about why you had to come in early?" Dr. Singh asks.

I explain our plan. I talk for so long that my voice gets hoarse, but I keep going and tell him about what happened onstage at Carnegie Hall.

"I had an anxiety attack," I say, gripping my knees once they stop jiggling. "Aren't I not supposed to have those anymore? Isn't that why I'm seeing you, a psychiatrist? Why I'm on medication?"

"Well," Dr. Singh begins, "Noah, this new medication has been working for you up until now, but that doesn't mean you'll stop having anxiety attacks completely. Will we possibly have to reevaluate again? Perhaps. Remember, treating anxiety disorders is an ongoing process. One you'll keep learning from. This incident doesn't mean that your treatment isn't working. It does not mean that you're failing."

"So, the results aren't instant," I say. My psychiatrist nods. "And my anxiety will never go away completely. But what you're telling me"—I swallow—"is that my anxiety disorder will continually get better?"

"Exactly," Dr. Singh confirms. "Noah, like I said in our first meeting, your circumstances are extraordinary. You also have generalized anxiety disorder, so you cannot fault yourself for having an anxiety attack."

"I should still be proud of my accomplishments." I gaze into the sky outside, watching the colors lie across Central Park and the surrounding skyscrapers. "In how far I'm coming with my treatment."

"Correct," Dr. Singh says, smiling at me. "Do you think you can do that?"

"Be proud of myself," I murmur, gazing out at the night sky beyond Dr. Singh's office windows. "Yeah. I think I can do that."

CHAPTER FORTY-FIVE
DAISY

The day of our Juilliard auditions, the early morning March cold seeps through my dress when Noah and I step outside. We match, both all in black.

I spent the night at his apartment again because it's closer to Carnegie Hall than Brooklyn. My parents agreed because Mazhar and Amal stayed, too. I told them we were having a slumber party to help with our nerves.

I woke up to a text from my mom:

Ma (7:07 a.m.): Good luck today. Call us when you're done. Ti voglio bene, Daisy. We all do.

She's trying. They both are. And I'll take that over them not owning up to our issues.

My heart pounds in my chest the entire Lyft ride to

Carnegie Hall. Douglas is waiting for us outside, keys to the performance hall in one hand, a coffee cup in the other. Gavin is standing next to him, bags of equipment across his shoulders.

"What the hell?" Noah screeches as his brother seizes him in a tight hug. "Gavin! When did you get here? How long are you staying? Do Mom and Dad—"

"I got in last night," Gavin admits sheepishly, smacking Noah's back with another hug. "Mom and Dad know, yeah. But I said I'd wait until tonight to see them, just to avoid spoiling the surprise."

"What are you doing here?" Noah breathes as Gavin gives me a hug, introducing himself to everyone.

"Well, obviously, I'm not going to let Douglas film your video alone, now am I? He's a better editor than me, sure, but he can't center a frame to save his life." Gavin laughs, dodging Douglas's elbow jab. "C'mon, then. Let's get inside."

We walk into the splendor of the Stern Auditorium. Even though Noah and I are on its stage once again, the familiarity of unpacking our instruments, running chunks of rosin along our bows, tuning our strings, running through our scales, it all seems normal.

The only things that are completely out of place are the camera Gavin's attaching to the tripod and the mic Douglas is setting up next to a laptop on his knees.

"Are you ready?" Bravado laces Douglas's question. Mazhar

and Amal watch us from their plush, ruby-red seats in the front row.

Noah and I gaze at each other. The stage lights above our heads are just as warm as the ones at our academy, and that's a comfort.

"Yeah." I smile down the length of my violin.

We draw our bows across our separate strings, the deep sounds seeming to travel to the chandelier, which is still glowing beautifully.

"Good." Gavin gives us a thumbs-up from behind the camera, studying the viewfinder.

"We're going to count off, then give you the signal we're recording," Douglas explains, taking his place next to Gavin. "Then you start playing."

"You can do this," Amal tells us.

"Show the whole internet what you're capable of," Mazhar adds, taking Amal's hand in his.

Gavin counts down from three, his voice reverberating off the walls, lights, and chandelier above. Then Douglas points at us onstage.

We both take a collective breath like we share a pair of lungs and assume first position. Our fingers splayed across our boards, my violin under my chin, while Noah is curled around his cello, both of us looking at the camera.

Noah plucks his C and G strings, his fingers stiff as he moves. I join him by drawing my bow across my A string while he concentrates on lower notes. But even though we performed this exact same duet for our winter holiday concert, it feels different here, onstage at Carnegie Hall.

Now we know who the world thinks we are.

Now we're determined to prove them wrong.

I chance looking away from my violin to watch Noah, and as our song is reaching the part where violin and cello merge together, he's gazing at me. His glasses are at the edge of his nose, his curls rumpled against his forehead.

My braid splays undone against my shoulder.

We transition to a vibrato frenzied enough to make our fingers hurt, my left hand tightening around my bow as horsehair is freed from both of ours.

We bring the song to a close in a ringing of A and E strings that wraps around our bodies and seems to be absorbed into the very history of the performance hall itself.

Gavin and Douglas explode with cheers. Mazhar and Amal yell about how incredible we were. I walk over to Noah, both of our chests heaving as our fingers shake against our instruments.

"We did it," I whisper, adjusting his glasses for him.

"Yeah." Noah takes my hand in his before I move it away, his fingers brushing my violin.

I stretch up on my tiptoes to kiss him. Just once, even though I want to kiss him more. But there will be time for that later. "Thank you," I murmur, leaning my forehead against his. Our noses touching, our lips brushing against each other's. "Now, let's go." I smile at him. "We can't be late for our auditions."

Noah's brothers pack up their equipment, he and I pack up our instruments, and we head to Juilliard. My heart's beating through my chest and I can feel Noah's through his fingers the entire way to Lincoln Center.

When we walk inside, I take in the sunlight spilling patterns across the floor through the angular windows. We're completely alone, not even with the sound of strings being plucked somewhere as an accompaniment.

"Are you nervous?" Noah asks, and quickly shakes his head. "Silly question. Of course you are."

"No." I pull the ribbon from my hair and let it cascade down my shoulder. "I mean, I am. But I'm also really excited. How are you feeling?"

"Anxious." Noah lets go of my hand to brush his fingers through his hair. "But that's okay. I know that now." He takes a deep breath, one that I mirror. "I know we can do this."

He takes my hand in his again. My left fingers scrabble against his right knuckles.

"Good luck."

"Good luck."

We go to pull away from each other, but I raise our entwined hands to his cheek instead, running my knuckles along it. He smiles at me. Neither of us was ready to let go yet. "I love you, Noah."

He cups my face in his hands, his fingers gliding along my skin. "I love you, Daisy."

And he kisses me, in the middle of Juilliard, before we turn on our heels, listening to the music of each other's footsteps as we walk into our futures.

EPILOGUE, SEVEN MONTHS LATER
DAISY

We've been at Juilliard for nearly two months.

And I'm only just starting to believe it.

I even received a full scholarship, so I didn't have to use the money *The Hope Baker Hour* gave me after all. On my eighteenth birthday, I put it in a college fund for Holly instead so she won't have to worry as much as I did.

"It's Saturday; get out of your dorm!" Amal whines from FaceTime, Noah holding his phone up in the air as we lie sprawled out on his bed. His roommate, a violist named Sai, is seeing a movie with his boyfriend, so we have the place to ourselves. "Take us to see the leaves!"

"You *knew* California didn't have seasons like back home." Noah's laugh still manages to fill me up, even after almost a year of being together.

It hasn't seemed real, Mazhar and Amal living in California.

Daisy | 299

I know it's normal for friends to separate for college, but that doesn't make it any easier. I miss them both a little bit every day.

"Well, we can't change that now, can we?" Mazhar mutters, grinning. "It's not our fault California *suddenly* sees red leaves on a tree and calls it fall."

"Fine." I lean against Noah, his cardigan soft against my shoulder. "We'll go live when we get to the park. Okay?"

"We love you!" our friends chorus from across the country as they click out of FaceTime. The picture of Haggis sleeping that is Noah's phone background stares down at us instead.

"Are we bringing our instruments?" I ask Noah as he pulls me to my feet and into his arms, kissing the top of my head.

"Of course. See you in a minute?"

I cuddle into Noah for a second longer, leaving his dorm to head to mine and grab my violin, which I keep on top of the extra blankets I have for nights when Noah sneaks over to sleep in my dorm instead.

Getting a single room has more benefits than I originally thought.

We walk through Lincoln Center and board the M104 bus. I get settled in a seat with Noah standing in front of me, double-decker tourist buses and yellow taxis also choking the streets. He asks me about how the Halloween party preparations are going for St. Peregrine's.

I never went back to St. Vincent de Paul after Father Benedetti tried to pray my disability away. I started attending St. Peregrine's the Sunday after Noah and I moved into the dorms. It's been an adjustment, attending Mass without my family next to me in the same pew. But the congregation at St. Peregrine's has become a different sort of family. Sometimes, Noah joins me dressed in his kilt, me in a simple red dress. We both sit in the back, listening to Father Holt preach about God's love, never once drawing attention to the disabled members of the church.

Noah is not as religious as I am, but he says he likes the stories.

Other times, he'll use the hour I'm at Mass to visit his parents and walk Haggis, two things that seem to help him keep calm.

"Well," I begin, my violin case bouncing in my lap. "It's a Halloween party at a Catholic church. So, no scary costumes or anything. But Father Holt did okay a haunted house. There's going to be spaghetti and mushed-up grapes for brains, things like that." I laugh. "So, kind of corny, but still fun."

"Did your parents say they'd bring Holly?" Noah asks.

"They're thinking about it." I shrug. I've started seeing Dr. McBride at the same practice as Noah's psychiatrist. She's been helping me work through years of my parents' emotional neglect. I think they had a hard time with it at first. Our family doesn't believe in telling strangers their business. But they're coming around. They've even offered to go with me. But I told them therapy is something I have to do on my own for now, and they're actually respecting that. It's a slow process, but a rewarding one. "Still debating on whether the trip into Manhattan is worth it when she could just go trick-or-treating in the apartment building."

"Sure, she could." Noah readjusts his grip on the metal pole. "But you'd be there, *and* she gets candy. A double win, I think."

"Mind if I text them that?" I smile up at him, and he bends down to kiss me before we get off the bus and head into Central Park's Fifty-Ninth Street entrance. The one that we walk through every week now.

After our performance on the day of our auditions, the internet exploded again. Only this time, it wasn't because of some fairy tale the world decided to write about us. It got to the point where people were commenting on our video on the Moray Stage YouTube channel, asking when we'd be starting our own.

So, we started one. Gavin and Douglas taught us all we needed to know about video editing. Over time, the more videos we posted, the comments about how much of a burden I've overcome, about how I'm lucky Noah loves me, became less frequent. Sure, we still get some of that, but the love and excitement outweigh them by far.

Beaux even deleted his e7string account.

We perform songs together once a week and livestream those, too. We've taken to streaming from Central Park because we spend so much of our time studying inside. Which is why I now carry a tripod on one shoulder, and my violin case on the other.

We reach our favorite location: a section of rocks, still surrounded by dazzling red and orange leaves, looking out over the water, and get our instruments unpacked and ready. I open our YouTube account, anchor my phone to the tripod, and go live.

"Hey, everyone!" We grin into the camera, comments already pouring in, including a lot of heart and fall leaf emojis from Mazhar and Amal.

"Ready, Daisy?" Noah turns to me and I nod. He draws his bow across his strings, taking in the sound of his cello. "Perfect."

His eyes shine, and he kisses me again before he begins to play, letting each note rest on the leaves above our heads.

Positioning my violin under my chin, I come in a second later, knowing as we fill this park with music that in this moment, right now, nothing else matters.

Just me, him, and our strings.

ACKNOWLEDGMENTS

I knew that I wanted to be an author when I was seven years old, so I have plenty of people to thank for this.

First, my incredible agent, Emily Forney, and all of BookEnds Literary. Emily, thank you for your tireless love, kindness, guidance, and determination. To say that I adore you would be an understatement worthy of tears only Darcey Silva herself is capable of producing.

My amazing editor, Tiffany Colón, and the entirety of Scholastic. Going from loving the Scholastic Book Fair throughout my childhood to being published here has been a dream. Thank you for giving my orchestra kids their home, and for changing my life.

Reen Mikhail, for creating the best cover I could've ever imagined. To my book designer, Yaffa Jaskoll, and my production editor, Melissa Schirmer, for bringing Daisy and Noah's story into reality in such gorgeous detail. I am so grateful to have had each of you by my side.

Tia Bearden and Jessica Lemmons, my critique partners before Daisy and Noah were even thoughts in my mind. You've been there for me for all these years, believing in me when I had no belief in myself. I love you with all my heart. Thank you for loving me with all of yours.

Michelle Mohrweis, for being my critique partner, my agent sibling, and, most importantly, one of my best friends. I will forever be your late-night car companion whenever you need me. Thank you for being my rock throughout this entire process of having Daisy and Noah meet the rest of the world.

My critique partner Taylor Tracy, for calling me during a power outage, for writing beautiful books, and for your endless encouragement.

Cara Liebowitz, Gabe Moses, Kati Gardner, Lillie Lainoff, and Sabina Nordqvist, thank you for everything. Disabled authors are each other's community, and there aren't enough words to express how grateful I am that you were my introductions. I cannot wait to see what the future holds for all of us. (Broadway and hugs? Yes, Broadway and hugs.)

#TeamNoahsFamily: Briana Miano, Chelsea Abdullah, E.M. Anderson, Eva Seyler, Libby Kennedy, and Morgan Matich. For loving the Moray family before anyone else. Thank you for Soft Dad Lewis, the #TeamGavin needlepoint, and the Haggis appreciation.

Daniel Aleman, instantaneous friendships are rare, and I am forever grateful for ours.

Jonny Garza Villa, for the promise of creating a literary cinematic universe together and for our friendship, the start of which neither of us can remember.

Rachel Lynn Solomon, your early eyes on this book and incredibly kind words were such a comfort. (I've kept that note where you cheer on Daisy and Noah, by the way.)

Julian Winters, I had no idea you were watching my journey, and to learn that touched my heart. I hope I've made you proud!

Ashley Schumacher, Bethany Mangle, Brittany Machado, Caitlin Colvin, Erin Grammar, Kelsey B. Toney, Kristin Lambert, Lucy Mason, and Mary Lynne Gibbs, for celebrating with me.

Eric Rittle, Leah Rittle, and Dr. Mert Keçeli, thank you for gathering me in. For the movies and barbecue in Times Square, dramatic readings at the Strand, and so much more. (An extra thank you to Mert for answering my questions about Turkish culture, Islam, and medicine.) Our bond is one of my favorite things in this world, because every time I go into Manhattan, I come home to you.

Brenna Kyner, Dylan Mottaz, Gwen Yannayon, Morgan Vorpahl, Shannah Doerner, and Val Kapetanovic, I cannot wait for the Cute Crew's next adventure! Pamela Núñez Trejo, I'm so grateful our love for Shirayuki and Zen brought us together in the middle of artist alley.

Aisha Wallis; Chris Stuckmann; Leanne and Callum Simpson; Kelly Martin; Rachel Isaacson; Renee Thomas; and Shala Haslam, to put it simply, thank you for your friendships.

To my family, you always knew this would happen. I love you!

Lastly, to the disabled readers who found themselves in Daisy and Noah. I hope you feel seen and know just how worthy of love you are.

ABOUT THE AUTHOR

Melissa See is a disabled author of young adult contemporary romances. When not writing, she can be found reading, baking, or curled up with her cat, most likely watching anime or *90 Day Fiancé*. She currently lives in the New York countryside. *You, Me, and Our Heartstrings* is her debut novel.